DANCE DIVAS

Showtime!

DANCE DIVAS

Showtime!

Two to Tango
(coming soon)

DANCE DIVAS
Showtime!

Sheryl Berk

BLOOMSBURY
NEW YORK   LONDON   NEW DELHI   SYDNEY

First published in the United States of America in September 2013
by Bloomsbury Children's Books
www.bloomsbury.com

For information about permission to reproduce selections from this book, write to
Permissions, Bloomsbury Children's Books, 1385 Broadway, New York, New York 10018
Bloomsbury books may be purchased for business or promotional use. For information on
bulk purchases please contact Macmillan Corporate and Premium Sales Department at
specialmarkets@macmillan.com

Library of Congress Cataloging-in-Publication Data
Berk, Sheryl.
Showtime! / by Sheryl Berk.
pages   cm. — (Dance Divas ; #1)
Summary: Drama ensues for the Dancing Divas, a team of eight- to twelve-year-old girls
who live to dance, as they rehearse in the studio and travel all around competing for titles.
ISBN 978-1-61963-181-6 (paperback) • ISBN 978-1-61963-182-3 (hardcover)
ISBN 978-1-61963-183-0 (e-book)
[1. Dance teams—Fiction. 2. Dance—Fiction.] I. Title.
PZ7.B45236Sh 2013   [Fic]—dc23   2013006300

Book design by Donna Mark
Typeset by Westchester Book Composition
Printed and bound in the U.S.A. by Thomson-Shore Inc., Dexter, Michigan
2 4 6 8 10 9 7 5 3 1 (paperback)
2 4 6 8 10 9 7 5 3 1 (hardcover)

All papers used by Bloomsbury Publishing, Inc., are natural, recyclable products
made from wood grown in well-managed forests. The manufacturing processes
conform to the environmental regulations of the country of origin.

To my beautiful ballerina, Carrie.
Oh my gooshness . . .
I love you to the moon and the stars!

Table of Contents

CHAPTER 1

Step to It

Scarlett Borden wrapped her waist-long wavy red hair into a tight ballerina bun and secured it into place with about a dozen hairpins. She checked every angle of her hair in the dressing-room mirror and tucked a stubborn curly strand behind her ear, hoping it would stay there. That loose curl was all Miss Toni would need to see and she'd go ballistic ("Sloppy hair equals sloppy feet!"). With only three days left to the City Lights dance competition in New York City, her dance coach's nerves were on edge. Something as minor as a stray curl could easily set her off.

"Look out, there's a storm brewing," Scarlett's best friend—and Dance Divas teammate—Rochelle Hayes said, swinging her dance bag off her shoulder and tossing it on a bench. She'd just come from her solo rehearsal and was dripping in sweat, or as Miss Toni preferred to call it, "glowing."

"What happened *now*, Rock?" Scarlett asked. "Please don't tell me you forgot your *pointe* shoes again?"

"I told Toni, I do much better barefoot!" she protested, demonstrating a graceful *grand jeté*. "She freaked the minute I walked in the door barefoot."

Scarlett sighed. "Of course she freaked! She gave you three warnings."

"*Pointe* shoes hurt!" Rochelle groaned, rubbing her toes. "And I showed her I could do it. She threw the sheet music on the floor!"

Scarlett knew her friend was playing with fire. The last time any student had disagreed with Miss Toni—much less refused to wear her costume choice (even the giant pineapple hat for the hula number)—she not only got cut from the group number but was also asked to leave the studio . . . forever. There were tons of dance studios in New Jersey, but few that had Dance Divas' reputation.

"Rock, you're my rock," Scarlett said, and put her arm around her friend. "I need you on this team." How many times had her BFF come to her rescue when she was feeling frustrated or freaked out over a dance routine?

"You're always there for me," Scarlett insisted. "What about the time the giant spinning teacup in our 'Tea for Two' duet got stuck? You totally saved the day!"

"I pushed it," Rochelle said, then shrugged. "It was nothing."

"It was *something*, which is why I am repaying the favor. I am not letting you get kicked off this team!"

She dug Rochelle's *pointe* shoes out of her bag and handed them to her. They looked brand new, probably because Rochelle had refused to break them in. "Please, I'm begging you, just put on the toe shoes for group rehearsal."

"Fine!" Rochelle replied. "But for you, not for Toni. My mom says she's crazy."

Scarlett nodded. Yup, there was no doubt that Antoinette "Toni" Moore was nuts. All the students at Dance Divas Studio in Scotch Plains, New Jersey, knew it. But they also knew that she won national championships. She got kids into music videos, and four of her older students had landed jobs on Broadway in just the past year alone. If you wanted to be a professional dancer one day, this was the only studio in the tristate area worth going to.

Plenty of Scarlett's classmates at Whitley Middle School commuted an hour into New York City to study with preprofessional ballet troupes and wondered why Scarlett refused to leave Dance Divas. Maybe it was because Miss Toni saw something more in her than just a ballerina on a *barre*. She pulled emotions out of her that Scarlett didn't even know she had. When Scarlett performed one of the lyrical or contemporary numbers Toni choreographed for her, she felt like she was flying across the stage and exploding like Fourth of July fireworks with every leap and acrobatic flip.

"Dance is making magic every time you step on that stage," Toni told her. And Scarlett believed it. None of the other ballet classes she'd taken since she was two had ever done this for her. Even though Toni drove her crazy, they had a connection; they understood each other.

But some girls on her dance team accused her of being Miss Toni's pet, especially Liberty Montgomery, the new girl who had joined the team in September. She could dance anything Toni threw at her: modern, lyrical, tap, Irish step. Liberty was a one-girl dance recital.

"You sickled your foot!" Liberty protested the last time they had been assigned to a trio together. She demonstrated how Scarlett accidentally rolled her ankle inward. "And you're a beat behind me and Rochelle. You're a disaster."

Liberty was in fact even harder to please than Miss Toni.

"It's not just you; it could be any of us," Rochelle assured her. "That girl just hates to have anyone stand in the way of her spotlight."

Rochelle had her own issues with Liberty, which started the first day she arrived at the studio.

"You do hip-hop, right?" she asked Rochelle.

Rochelle nodded. "Yeah, I've taken hip-hop for a long time."

"My mom says hip-hop is like the diet soda of dance. It's not the real thing." Liberty smirked. "And my mother is a big Hollywood choreographer, so she would know. A few pops and locks do not a dancer make."

Rochelle fumed. "I do a lot more than just pop and lock!" She demonstrated a smooth jazz-funk move across the floor.

"What do you call that?" Liberty asked.

"It's krumping, and a little freestyle," Rochelle explained.

"It's ridiculous," Liberty said. "It requires absolutely no technique or talent whatsoever."

"Then you do it!" Rochelle shot back.

"And make you look worse than you already do?" Liberty grinned. "My mom always tells me to be kind to people who are less fortunate."

Scarlett had to admit that despite Liberty's attitude problem, her mom did have a pretty impressive résumé.

"She choreographed Adele's last video," Scarlett pointed out.

"Says who?" Rochelle asked.

"Well, Liberty told me—"

"Scarlett, she lies. A lot."

Bria Chang, their other teammate, strolled into the dressing room, her *pointe* shoes hanging from ribbons around her neck. Her head was buried in a pre-algebra textbook.

"Bria, you think Liberty is a big show-off, don't you?" Rochelle asked.

"Did I miss something? I always miss something!" Bria sighed. "I've got this test in math tomorrow, and I am seriously gonna fail it."

"We were just talking about Liberty's mom

and how she's a big Hollywood choreographer," Scarlett explained.

"Supposedly . . . ," Rochelle chimed in. "I don't believe anything that comes out of Liberty's mouth."

"Well, there's one way to find out for sure," Bria said, opening her laptop and searching "Jane Montgomery" on it.

"Sorry, Rock . . ." Bria showed her the Wikipedia page. "It says she did Adele's video, a couple for Katy Perry—"

"Okay, so she's not lying . . . this time. That doesn't make Liberty the world's greatest dancer, does it?" Rochelle asked.

Scarlett suspected that having a famous choreographer for a mother was part of the problem. Mrs. Montgomery was often at the studio, peeking through the windows and watching Liberty rehearse. Afterward, she'd pull her aside and whisper in her ear. Whatever she said, it must not have been good, because one time, Liberty ran past her into the bathroom, sobbing.

"I think Liberty's mom puts a lot of pressure on her," Scarlett told her teammates.

"Well, my mom puts a lot of pressure on me!" Bria piped up. "She said if I fail this math test Friday, I'm grounded for life!"

Bria was always struggling with one subject or another. On more than one occasion, her parents had threatened to pull the plug on her competing with Dance Divas.

"How did you do on the Spanish quiz yesterday?" Scarlett asked. "*¿Muy bueno?*"

"I don't even know what you just said, so how do you think I did?" Bria moaned, scooping her long glossy black hair into a ponytail. "If I don't get at least a B on this math test, that's it—no City Lights this weekend. And my mom means it!"

"Do NOT let Toni hear you say that," Rochelle said, then shivered. "She will freak if you drop out last minute."

"I know. And with all these rehearsals, I have no time to study! What am I going to do?" Bria looked desperate.

Just then, Scarlett noticed the clock on the dressing-room wall.

"OMG, it's four thirty-three!" she screamed, grabbing Rochelle and Bria by the hand and pulling them with her. "We're late for rehearsal by three minutes. She's going to have our heads!"

CHAPTER 2
Practice Makes Perfect

Scarlett, Rochelle, and Bria bounded into studio 2 just as Toni was taking her place in the front of the room. Liberty, of course, was already at the *barre*, warming up. The girl was a human pretzel; she could bend and twist in every direction! Her shiny blond hair was pulled back in a braid. *Ugh*, Scarlett thought, tucking a stray strand behind her ear again, *I wish I had straight silky hair like that!* She also noticed Liberty's custom dance outfit: a hot-pink cropped mesh top and matching shorts with the word "STAR" bedazzled on the butt. Scarlett looked down at her black leotard and pink leg warmers and wrapped her arms over her chest. She felt positively plain and boring standing next to Liberty.

"Nice of you to join us, ladies," Toni snapped.

Then she gave them "the look." Scarlett knew it well—she actually had nightmares about it sometimes. It said, "You have disappointed me; you are dead meat!" all in a single icy-cold stare.

The strange thing was that Toni was beautiful. She had porcelain-white skin, wavy dark hair that fell softly around her shoulders, and pale-blue eyes. Scarlett's little sister, Gracie, thought she looked like Snow White.

"More like the Evil Queen," Rochelle had said, chuckling. "There is nothing princess-like about her."

But Scarlett could see it: Toni had once been a kinder, gentler person. She'd even watched some of Toni's old performances on YouTube, when she was just Antoinette Moore, a young teen dancer at American Ballet Company, floating across the stage in *The Nutcracker* to the "Waltz of the

Flowers." This was not the same woman who stood before them, day after day, stamping her foot on the wood floor and barking orders. Even with Toni's hair pulled into a severe bun and her signature bright-red lipstick, Scarlett could see there was something *soft* about her.

"I want to see perfect *pirouettes piqué*." Toni's voice brought Scarlett back to attention. "Shoulders down! How many times do I have to correct you? We have three days, and this number is a big hot mess! Scarlett, front and center!"

Scarlett obeyed, taking her place in front of the other girls.

"Miss Toni! I can't see with Scarlett's big butt blocking my view," Liberty complained.

"Well, there's nothing to see," Toni replied. "You should know this number cold by now without having to follow me. Five-six-seven-eight . . ."

They rehearsed for two hours without a break. The number was a strange contemporary piece set to the *tap-tap-tap* sounds of a computer keyboard. No music; just strange computer blips and bells. Onstage, there would be a giant video screen behind them, projecting fake e-mails and text messages. The routine was called, "Cyberbully," and in it, Scarlett played the victim of mean girls bugging her online.

"I want to see the pain in your face," Toni instructed her, "as if these words are like knives cutting into you."

Scarlett winced. That wasn't hard to imagine. All she had to do was recall some of Liberty's nastiest insults.

Scarlett flitted from girl to girl, trying to escape their clawing arms. It was dramatic and unsettling.

Toni seemed satisfied. "If this doesn't win Saturday, I give up," she said under her breath.

At the end of rehearsal, she gathered the girls around her in a huddle, like a football coach handing out plays to his team. "I want you to know that Saturday's competition is going to be tough," she began. "Some of the best studios are coming to compete, and we cannot afford to make any mistakes. Is that clear?"

Scarlett was used to the speech. It always began with something like "Don't mess up!" and ended with "Do I make myself clear?" To Toni, every competition was a matter of life and death, because her reputation was riding on it. But what she forgot was that none of the girls liked to lose either. It felt awful to spend dozens of hours on group routines, solos, and combinations, only to be handed a second- or third-place trophy. Every one of them wanted to win first place—in every category.

"I said, *is that clear?*" Toni boomed. Four heads nodded. "We leave for the city at eight a.m."

Liberty raised her hand. "Miss Toni, Saturday is my eleventh birthday, and my mom was planning on having a party for some family and VIP friends later in the day. I think maybe a countess and . . ."

Toni placed a hand dramatically over her eyes, as if to block out Liberty from her vision altogether. "I don't care if Queen Elizabeth herself is coming to tea at your house. You'll be there!" She said each word with the razor-sharpness of a *battement* at the *barre*. "Is. That. Clear?"

Liberty gulped. It was the first time Scarlett had ever seen her know-it-all teammate at a loss for words.

Toni turned and faced the rest of the group. "That goes for all of you. Anyone who is not interested in following my rules . . . there's the door." She pointed to the studio exit. "I don't care if you like me, and I don't care if you like one another. But we are a team, and we act like one. We let nothing stand in our way of winning."

On that note, Toni walked out the door, leaving the girls to think about what she'd said.

"My mom is not going to be happy." Liberty sighed. "She called the caterer and everything."

"Give me a break." Rochelle groaned.

"Nothing like team spirit," Scarlett said. "Can we all just try to get along?"

"Oh, and who appointed you cheer captain?" Liberty shot back. "After I win the crown for Junior Solo this weekend, I'll be Toni's favorite—not you."

"I wouldn't be so sure about that," Rochelle

said, defending her BFF. "Unless they give out prizes for the biggest mouth. In that case, you'll win for sure."

Liberty bristled. "At least I have a solo. Toni cut yours this week. I wonder why? Maybe because you *stink?*"

"Not as bad as your feet stink!" Rochelle shot back, holding her nose.

"Aw, someone's a sore loser! What's the matter? Miss Toni thought you weren't good enough to compete?"

"Liberty, cut it out!" Scarlett cried. "It's none of your business. Stop or I'll—"

"You'll what? You'll run to Miss Toni and rat me out? Aw, I'm really scared." She picked up her ballet shoes and waved them in Scarlett's face, taunting her. "See ya Saturday, girls," she said, and smirked. "I can't wait."

Scarlett had a sinking feeling in her stomach that this weekend wasn't going to go as smoothly as planned.

CHAPTER 3

Big Apple Bound

Just as Miss Toni had promised, the Dance Divas' bus pulled up in front of the studio at 8:00 a.m. sharp. It was hard to miss the studio, even from a mile away. There was a bright gold sign on the roof and a giant pair of pink ballet slippers in a star. Miss Toni had personally designed the logo.

Scarlett's dance bag weighed a ton and was digging into her shoulder. Meanwhile, her mom had both hands full, lugging a duffel filled with costumes, makeup, and hair tools outside to the curb.

"I feel like I'm forgetting something," her mom, Hillary, said to Bria's mother, Aimi. "I know

I packed the curling iron and the blow-dryer, but did I bring the flat iron?"

"I have an extra one if you need it," Aimi assured her. "I always bring two in case one breaks."

"Or someone like me forgets," Hillary said with a chuckle. "I swear, I'd forget my head if it wasn't bobby-pinned to my shoulders!"

Bria rolled her eyes. "My mom, she is so perfect," she whispered to Scarlett. "She never forgets anything. Not the capital of Wisconsin. Not the formula for finding the area of a trapezoid . . ."

"I guess your math test didn't go so well?" Scarlett tried to sympathize.

"I won't get the grade until Monday. Which is probably the only reason I am allowed to compete this weekend." Bria sighed. "She doesn't care about my dancing. She just wants me to get straight As like she did her whole life. She was so smart that she skipped two grades and went to college when she was sixteen!"

"I bet your mom would never do a dive front walkover like you!" Scarlett reminded her. "Or twenty-five *pirouettes* in a row. You're amazing!"

Bria shrugged. "My older sister, Lily, is amazing. She got to go to the New Jersey state senate last year and read an essay she wrote about serving chocolate milk in school cafeterias. When she grows up, she wants to be a journalist like my dad, covering wars and politics and stuff. It's not easy being in my family!" She held a stack of textbooks in her left arm and her laptop in her right. "I have two hours till we get to New York. I *have* to study."

Scarlett glanced over at Mrs. Chang. She didn't seem "bossy" like Bria said. In fact, she was smiling sweetly and helping Scarlett's mom double-check their bags.

Scarlett was glad her mom didn't pressure her—not to get perfect grades and not to win dance titles. She was anything *but* a stage mom. "You do your very best—that is all I can ever ask for," she told her and her little sister, Gracie. "I'll always be proud of you if you try your hardest."

Her parents were divorced, which Scarlett knew made things diffi⬛or them as a family. Her dad now lived in Manhattan ⬛ her mom had to juggle a full-time job as a teacher and full-time parenting. Scarlett liked to think that she was pretty independent. She could take care of herself, even make her own breakfast (Eggo waffles in the toaster) if her mom was too busy.

But Gracie was a whole other story. Ever since the divorce, she was super clingy and super annoying.

"Scoot, can you play Barbies with me?" she'd plead, right as Scarlett was trying to get her social studies homework done before dance class. She always called her Scoot—ever since she was a baby and couldn't pronounce her full name. Scarlett hated the nickname, but it stuck.

"Not now—I have to finish this." She tried to close her bedroom door, but Gracie pushed back in. "Mama's busy. I wanna play Olympics with the Barbies. Pleeeeeeeease?"

Scarlett was sorry whenever she gave in. It meant an hour of tossing Barbies in the air and watching Gracie pose them in splits and hand-stands.

"This is the front pike somersault my coach showed us last week!" Gracie said. She kept the doll's legs straight and flipped her over. "Put your arm out—you're the beam!" she instructed Scarlett.

"Uh-huh." Scarlett yawned. She knew Gracie loved being on the Mini Sparklers in her gymnastics school, but to her, it was playtime. Gracie loved the shiny red, white, and blue leotards and swinging on the rings. At every gymnastics class, she would race around the mats, tumbling and flipping every which way. Her coach called her "the Jumping Bean" because Gracie could never stand still.

"She's a diamond in the rough," Coach Maggie told her mom. "She has so much natural talent and ability. But she doesn't want it badly enough to take it seriously."

Scarlett understood what that meant. She knew lots of girls at Dance Divas who were naturally graceful and talented. Some had beautiful turnouts, pointed toes, and straight legs. But that was only part of it. To be on a competition team, to work with Miss Toni, you had to want it *badly*. You had to eat, sleep, and breathe Dance Divas. It took so much dedication, determination, and concentration that everything else faded into the background. Sometimes Scarlett was exhausted and fed up, but she pushed herself to nail a routine or take an extra stretch class. Miss Toni expected only the best, and Scarlett expected it from herself.

"I am as good as those big girls on the Elite Sparklers team," Gracie told Scarlett. "Better! I could win a gold medal if they just gave me a chance. I can even do this . . ." She twisted her Barbie's leg into a wide split until it accidentally popped out of the socket.

"I hope you don't do a split like *that*," Scarlett teased. "Ouch!"

Gracie's face turned bright red. "You broke my favorite Barbie!" she wailed, sending her mom racing into the room to referee.

"Did not!" Scarlett countered. "You broke her. I was just sitting here—"

"Mama, she's so mean!" her little sister sobbed, cradling the legless doll in her arms. "Look what she did!"

Her mom scooped Gracie up in her lap and gently stroked her hair. "Shhhh," she whispered. "It's okay. We can put a Band-Aid on Barbie and she'll be all better."

As she was searching through the first-aid kit in the medicine cabinet for bandages, she scolded Scarlett. "You're eleven and your little sister is only seven. Can't you just play nicely?" Her mom sighed.

It was no use trying to explain or defend herself. Gracie always won.

"Just imagine how hard it must be to be your kid sister," her mother told her. "You're a hard act to follow, honey." She pointed to a shelf in her bedroom, lined with crowns and trophies from dance competitions over the years. "Try and understand that Gracie just wants some attention, too. She wants to be you, Scarlett."

CHAPTER 4

Grace Face

It sounded crazy at the time, but when Gracie set her alarm for 6:30 Saturday morning to see her off, Scarlett suspected her mother might be right.

"Oh my gooshness!" Gracie said, fingering a red sequin leotard. She had this really irritating habit of combining words into her own "Gracie language" whenever she felt like it: like "Oh my goodness" and "Oh my gosh!" equaled "Oh my gooshness!"

"Careful!" Scarlett snapped, snatching the costume out of her hands. "You might tear it."

"I won't!" Gracie continued rummaging through the suitcases, undoing all the packing Scarlett and her mom had done the night before.

"What's this one for?" she asked, pulling out a light-blue chiffon dress. The skirt tiers looked like flower petals.

"My solo. It's called 'In the Clouds.'"

Gracie nodded. "It looks like the sky—or Cinderella's dress. Can I wear it sometime?"

Scarlett thought for a moment. Miss Toni never wanted them to wear a costume in competition more than once. "Sure, after City Lights, you can have it."

"Really?" Gracie leaped off the bed and did a cartwheel.

"Wow! That's pretty impressive. You're getting good at gymnastics!" Scarlett laughed. "Miss Toni would probably love a couple of those acro moves in our dances."

Gracie raised an eyebrow. "She would? You think? Maybe I could be in Dance Divas, too?"

Scarlett had never considered that her little

sister might be a dancer as well. Gracie loved gymnastics and tae kwon do classes. But ballet? Jazz? Lyrical? And she was *never* serious. Her mom insisted it was because she was only seven, but Scarlett knew their difference in attitude ran deeper than that.

They sort of looked like sisters: Scarlett had her mom's unkempt curly red hair and freckles, and Gracie had stick-straight, strawberry-blond hair that she got from her dad. But Scarlett loved watching any talent competition show—*Dancing with the Stars, American Idol, The X Factor*—whereas Gracie could sit staring at shows on Animal Planet for hours. And if Scarlett felt like sushi (her fave) for dinner, Gracie insisted on peanut butter and ketchup on a hot dog bun. She was the only seven-year-old Scarlett knew who ate breakfast, lunch, and dinner on a hot dog bun.

Scarlett's mom let Gracie get away with it— even if it was incredibly gross—because of the divorce.

"I think Gracie misses your dad," she confided

in Scarlett. "Hot dogs remind her of the back-yard barbecues we always had on Sundays."

Scarlett missed her dad, too. But there was no way she was going to eat scrambled eggs or ham and cheese on a hot dog bun. If she tried to talk about it with Gracie, her little sis quickly changed the subject.

"You doing okay, Grace Face?" Scarlett asked her one day when they were setting the table for dinner.

"What do you mean?" Gracie asked.

"I just mean, how are you feeling?"

Gracie scratched her head. "Michaela in my class got strep throat and Randy in gymnastics has broccoli-itis."

"You mean bronchitis," Scarlett said, and chuckled.

"Whatever," Gracie said, putting out the sil-verware.

"I didn't mean how is your health. I meant how are you doing with the whole divorce thing."

Gracie winced every time anyone mentioned

the "D" word. Maybe she thought that if no one talked about it, it never really happened.

"You know you can talk to me, right?" Scarlett offered, trying to sound very big sisterly. "If you have any questions or stuff?"

Gracie grinned. "What's the world's record for the most hot dogs eaten in ten minutes?"

Scarlett frowned. "Not those kinds of questions."

"You just don't know the answer," Gracie taunted her. "I do! It's one hundred ten!"

Scarlett's mom put her in charge of Gracie whenever she had to work late.

"Just let her stay at the dance studio with you," her mom pleaded. "Just for a few hours. She can sit outside and watch."

Scarlett knew what that meant. Gracie would press her nose against the studio windows, cross her eyes, stick out her tongue, and do whatever else she could think of to distract Scarlett. Luckily, Miss Toni was always too focused on correcting the dancers' technique to notice the little girl using her princess lip gloss to write "SCOOT!" on the window backward.

Gracie was an expert at driving her crazy, but occasionally Scarlett liked a challenge.

"Betcha can't do this!" Gracie teased, holding her leg in a heel stretch and hopping around in a circle.

Scarlett lifted her left leg perfectly vertical to her body. Her move was fluid and graceful. "Miss Toni calls this 'développé to the side,'" she explained.

"No hopping?" Gracie asked.

"No. No hopping."

"Well, that's not fun," she said. "Maybe I don't want to be part of your Dumb Divas team."

But once again, Scarlett thought that maybe she did. Maybe her mom was right and Gracie did want to be like her. She looked at her sister, oohing and ahhing over the costumes, and felt momentarily bad for constantly complaining and calling her "Grace Face."

Then Gracie stuck out her tongue and grabbed a pair of pink panties from the suitcase. She put them on her head and twirled around the room like a whirling top, wrecking everything in her path.

"Mom!" screamed Scarlett. "Gracie is being crazy again!"

Her mother came into the room wearing the same clothes she'd had on last night. She looked exhausted. A few red sequins were stuck in her auburn curls. "Girls, please, keep it down to a dull roar. I went to bed at three a.m. I haven't had my coffee yet."

"Did you finish the costume for the trio?" Scarlett asked hopefully.

"Yes, I finished. I think I must have hot-glued about a million sequins on that thing. Did we really need the entire bodice blinged out?"

Scarlett nodded. "You know what Toni says: 'Bling's the thing.'"

"You're supposed to be a girls' dance team, not the Rockettes," her mother said, and sighed. Then she noticed Gracie was wearing underpants on her head.

"New hat, munchkin?" she teased, pulling them off and tossing them back into Scarlett's bag.

"I don't wanna stay home with Grams and Poppy," Gracie whined. "Why can't I go, too?"

"Because Miss Toni has rules," Scarlett reminded her. "No siblings on the bus or backstage. But you're going to come to the show with Dad, Grams, and Poppy to cheer for us, right?"

Gracie shrugged. "Yes. But you're gonna have all the fun."

CHAPTER 5

All Aboard!

"Fun" wasn't exactly how Scarlett would have described the scene outside the studio. It was tense and chaotic. Toni was pacing anxiously. She looked like a volcano about to erupt.

"I said eight a.m. sharp. Where are Liberty and Rochelle?" she shouted.

She was reaching for her cell phone to call them when a long black stretch limo pulled up. Out stepped Liberty and her mom, Jane. They were wearing sunglasses and matching pink faux-fur jackets. Mrs. Montgomery had glossy long blond hair just like Liberty. *They could be twins,* Scarlett thought—give or take thirty years.

"OMG, is she kidding?" Bria gasped. "What a show-off!"

Mrs. Montgomery kiss-kissed the other mothers on both cheeks before setting her sights on Toni.

"We're here!" she exclaimed, throwing her arms out for a hug. The dance coach took a big step backward and glared.

"You're late. No one is late for a dance competition. You of all people, Jane, should understand that show business waits for no one. Not even you and your daughter. I would have thought you would be more professional."

Mrs. Montgomery stopped grinning. *Uh-oh*, Scarlett thought to herself, *those were fighting words!*

"Are you calling me unprofessional?" Mrs. Montgomery hissed. "I have choreographed dozens of music videos. I have worked with Madonna!" Her face turned bright red.

"Mom, please, I told you she was tough," Liberty whispered, trying to hold her mother back.

"She looks like a ferocious pink grizzly bear," Bria said, and chuckled. "This is so good! I have to post pics on Instagram!"

"Let it go, Mommy," Liberty pleaded. She knew better than to make Miss Toni mad.

"Yes." Toni smiled. "Let it go. Because if you don't, your daughter won't go to City Lights today."

"Ha! As if you'd pull a dancer out of a group number at the last minute!" Mrs. Montgomery tossed back.

"I would . . . I have . . . and I will." Toni had nerves of steel. She didn't flinch.

Scarlett's mom stepped between the two women.

"Ladies, ladies, can we please calm down and behave like grown-ups?" she pleaded.

As a third-grade teacher, she knew how to break up fights in the schoolyard. Still, Scarlett worried that her mother was in over her head this time.

"She started it!" Liberty's mom protested. *Well, that sounds like a third grader!* Scarlett thought.

"And now it's time to finish it," Scarlett's mom insisted. "Please? For the kids' sake?"

"Fine." Mrs. Montgomery sniffed. "I've worked with plenty of difficult people in my day. What's one more?"

"Tell them about the time that famous pop star wanted to wear red platform shoes, and they clashed with her outfit," Liberty said. Scarlett wasn't sure if she was bragging (as usual) or trying to distract her mom from Toni.

"Oh, what a nightmare!" Mrs. Montgomery began. "I told her that she looked ridiculous. Like Dorothy in *The Wizard of Oz*. But did she listen to me? *Nooooooo!*"

"Where would you like these, madam?" the limo driver asked.

Mrs. Montgomery hated to be interrupted—especially when she was telling a story that starred her and some famous celebrity. "You can put the luggage in there, Raymond." She motioned to the bus. "Don't forget the light-up makeup mirror."

"And my poodle pillow pet!" Liberty added. "Don't forget Fifi!"

Raymond took several bags in each hand and flung two over his neck. He huffed and puffed his way up the bus steps—with a stuffed pink poodle on his head.

Toni was willing to drop the argument as well. She had bigger things to worry about.

"Where is Rochelle?" she bellowed. "This bus leaves in five minutes—with or without her!"

CHAPTER 6

"Rock" and Roll

"Wait! Wait! We're here! We're here!" called a voice from the parking lot. It was Rochelle, and she was racing for the bus, her mom trailing behind her.

"I am so, so sorry," her mother, Jada, said, trying to catch her breath. "Rochelle's baby brother, Dylan, was up all night with a fever. I can't leave him. Hillary, would you mind if Rock bunked with you and Scarlett?"

Toni put her hands over her ears. It reminded Scarlett of something Gracie would do. She wondered if Miss Toni would throw a tantrum, too.

"I am not hearing this," Toni said slowly. "I am not hearing you tell me that you are sending your child to a competition without a parent chaperone."

"No, I didn't say that!" Mrs. Hayes tried to reassure her. "I said Hillary can watch her, right?"

Scarlett looked at her mom, who was completely caught off guard.

"Right, sure. Rock can stay with us in our hotel room," she said.

"There! Problem solved!" Mrs. Hayes added, pushing Rochelle toward the bus. "You girls go on. Kick some dance butts!"

"I'm sorry," Rochelle whispered to Scarlett. "I know it'll be crowded."

"Are you kidding? It'll be just like a slumber party in our hotel room!" Scarlett said.

Rochelle relaxed, but Toni was fuming. They were already fifteen minutes behind schedule. "All of you . . . on the bus!" she huffed.

The two-hour ride to New York City flew by. While Bria hit the books, the other girls played Name That Tune (Scarlett guessed One Direction's "What Makes You Beautiful" in just five notes) and finished with a game of Truth or Dare.

When it was Rochelle's turn, she chose "dare."

Liberty grinned: "I dare you to go up to Miss Toni and ask her, 'What's shakin', bacon?' "

"I can't. She'll kill me!" Rochelle exclaimed.

"You don't have to. You can take a dare back," Scarlett said, improvising, to protect her friend.

"A dare is a dare," Liberty taunted her. "Those are the rules. Unless you want to take it *for her?*"

Scarlett saw that Toni was sitting behind the driver, directing him through midtown traffic. Interrupting her was definitely not a good idea. But Rochelle was already in hot water with their dance coach. She couldn't let her make things worse.

"I'll do it," she said.

"No! Scarlett, you don't have to!" Rochelle tried to stop her. But it was too late. She was already inching her way toward the front of the bus.

"Miss Toni?" she asked timidly, tapping her on the shoulder.

"Yes?" Toni replied.

"Um, I have a question . . ."

"Well, what is it?"

Scarlett took a deep breath and blurted out, "What's shakin', bacon?"

Toni looked puzzled. Then she replied, "I'm the boss, applesauce. So go sit back down." She winked, and Scarlett heaved a huge sigh of relief.

As she took her seat next to Rochelle, she heard Liberty laughing hysterically. "I cannot believe you did that! Toni must think you're crazy!"

Scarlett bit her tongue. She was not about to take the bait again and talk back to Liberty. Her dad always told her there were certain people that enjoyed "getting you all fired up." Liberty was one of them.

"Ignore them," he advised. "If you do, they can't win."

So Scarlett said nothing as Liberty continued to crack up. Besides, the bus was pulling into the Millennium Broadway Hotel in Times Square.

"Check it out!" Rock pointed out the window. There was a huge neon marquee flashing, "WELCOME, CITY LIGHTS DANCERS!"

"We're here! We're here!" Bria bounced up and down in her seat. "This is awesome!"

Toni stood at the front of the bus and cleared her throat.

"Ladies and moms," she began. "Welcome to Times Square, New York City. The heart of Broadway theater, the center of the dance universe, where some of the most famous dancers in the world have performed."

The girls cheered and started naming their favorite Broadway shows: *Annie, Wicked, The Phantom of the Opera.*

Toni clapped her hands above her head, demanding full attention. Even the mothers became silent. "I want to remind you that from the minute you step off this bus and into that hotel, you represent Dance Divas Studio and you represent me. My reputation. You are proud, you are strong, and you let no one intimidate you. Is that clear?"

Everyone nodded.

"There are studios coming here whose goal is to beat us. Especially City Feet Dance Studio."

Scarlett raised her hand. "But they don't even know us. We've never competed against them."

"Well, we've never had a state title. Now we do, and trust me, they know us," Miss Toni said.

Bria was already searching for City Feet on her laptop. "I found their website. It says the studio is in Long Island, run by someone named Justine Chase, a former prima ballerina at American Ballet Company."

"Wait a sec; Miss Toni went to ABC," Scarlett said, grabbing the computer out of her hand. She looked at the photo of City Feet's dance coach: she was blond and petite, with a tiny beauty mark above her lip. Then she found a YouTube video of Toni's performance in *La Sylphide*. "Aha!" she cried. "I thought I remembered her. Look familiar?"

The girls squinted to watch the delicate dancer move right beside Miss Toni in a forest scene. She had the same platinum-blond hair, and there it was: the telltale mark above her lip.

"So you're saying Toni and Justine were ballerinas together way back when?" Liberty snickered. "Isn't that a co-inky-dink?"

"I don't think it's a coincidence. I think they want to beat each other," Scarlett concluded. "I think they're archenemies."

"Oooh." Bria giggled. "That sounds evil."

"Miss Toni can handle evil," Rochelle piped up. "I don't think we should be worrying about City Feet or Justine Chase."

Toni overheard the last part of the conversation. "Oh yes, you should be worried about City Feet. You know why? Because they're good. They're very good. We need to be better."

She checked her watch. "Okay, girls, we have three hours to practice before the competition. I reserved us a dressing room, and I want to run the group number and all the solos till they're perfect. I want everyone warmed up and ready to go in ten minutes."

And with that, the girls were off.

CHAPTER 7

Not-So-Lucky Stars

Those last three hours of rehearsal before a competition were the only time the girls had to iron out any wrinkles in a routine. It was also when Miss Toni liked to throw them a curve ball.

"I'm thinking we need to switch this up a little," she said, tapping her foot on the floor as she watched the group number. "Scarlett, I want you to start with a *rond de jambe attitude*. The rest of you follow. And a one and a two . . ."

Scarlett glanced over at Bria, who looked totally lost.

"It's too fast!" Bria whispered when they took a water break. "I can't learn it this quick! And I hate when she talks in French! Why can't ballet be in English?"

As they tried the number again, Bria did her best to keep up—to turn when Toni said *pirou ette*; to jump when she said *sauté*. She kept her back foot on the ground and her shoulders down. But her head was spinning as Toni called out: "Sharper! Sharper! Knees straight! Bria, you can do better than this! Focus!"

Bria spun out of control, right into Scarlett, who lost her balance and toppled out of a split handstand.

"I'm so sorry," Bria said, her eyes welling up. "I don't think I can do this."

"You can do it," Scarlett whispered. "We have to get through this."

"I guess it's not a competition until someone cries," Rochelle said.

Toni stopped the music and took Bria aside. "The judges are expecting flawless technique and precision," she said calmly. "I need to know that you are willing to work for that. No mishaps. No thoughts about anything except winning. Clear?"

Bria nodded and took her place once again behind Scarlett. This time, when Toni counted—"five-six-seven-eight"—she did a perfect *arabesque*.

At the end of the routine, Miss Toni applauded. "You girls nailed it. That was crisp, that was clean—that was a first-place win if I ever saw one!"

Backstage at the City Lights dance competition, the halls were packed with girls running their dances.

"Did you see some of those costumes?" Liberty asked her mom.

"I know." Her mother chuckled. "So tacky!"

Scarlett looked down at her blue chiffon dress. Her mother had sewn silver sequins all along the neckline. Was it tacky, too?

Rochelle read her thoughts. "It's beautiful, and your solo is amazing," she said, squeezing her friend's hand. "Go out there and win another title. For both of us, okay?"

"I'm sorry you don't get to perform your solo,"

Scarlett told her. "I know how hard you worked on it."

Rochelle shrugged. If there was one thing she had learned to do well from Toni, it was to "Toughen up." There would be other competitions, other chances to prove herself. The only thing that burned her was that Liberty got a solo this time.

"Just look at her. So full of herself!" Rochelle said.

"But that costume *is* gorgeous!" Bria sighed.

Liberty's mom had asked a friend—who just happened to be a designer for Lady Gaga—to create a one-of-a-kind blue-and-green-sequin leotard with real peacock feathers for a skirt.

"Stand still, Liberty!" her mom mumbled. Her mouth was filled with bobby pins to secure the headpiece, an emerald and sapphire tiara. "Stop fidgeting!"

Liberty's number was a contemporary jazz routine called "Wings." Scarlett had watched her do it over and over in rehearsals. There were tricks;

there were splits; there were thirty *fouetté pirouettes* with perfectly pointed toes (Liberty's specialty). It was what Toni called an "eyepopper showstopper," meaning the judges would be wowed.

By comparison, Scarlett's solo was mellower. The music was slow and gentle, like a soothing lullaby. Miss Toni told her it was about someone going to heaven, and she should dig deep and feel the emotion of it: the loss and the sadness as well as the beauty and the peace. So every time she danced it, she thought of the saddest day she could remember in her family: the day her grandpa Papa Eli—her dad's father—died on her eighth birthday. She missed him all the time—he was always in the front row at all of her dance recitals, and now she thought of him as her guardian angel. So standing backstage, waiting in the wings for her turn to dance, Scarlett said a little prayer: "Please, oh, please, let this be a great performance!"

Liberty's mom was fluffing one last feather when a voice boomed over the microphone: "And now, dancing a contemporary jazz routine entitled 'Wings,' please welcome from Dance Divas Studio . . . Liberty!"

Scarlett watched as her teammate strutted like a peacock out onto the stage. She nodded to the judges, then began her routine. If there was one thing Scarlett had to give her credit for, it was showmanship. She waved, she winked, she shook her hips, and shimmied her shoulders. By the end of the number, she had the entire audience on their feet for a standing ovation.

"That's my girl!" her mother squealed, hugging her as she came offstage. "You rocked it, baby!"

Scarlett gulped. Beating Liberty was not going to be easy.

"Okay, sugar muffin," her mom said. "Two more girls and then it's your turn. Time to get ready."

Scarlett made sure the straps of her dress were secure and that the delicate white lace bow in her hair was pinned in place.

"Do you have my lucky ballet shoes, Mom?" she asked, straightening the seams on her tights.

"I thought you had them, honey," her mom replied. "They're not with me. You must have left them in the dressing room."

But when they searched her bags, they were nowhere to be found.

"Rock, Bria—help me find them!" Scarlett began to panic. They looked in every bag, in every corner, under every pile of costumes.

"I don't get what the big deal is. Just wear another pair. You have at least six in your dance bag," Liberty said.

"No, it has to be *this* pair!" Scarlett answered. "You don't understand! I *need* my Lucky Stars shoes to win!"

Bria nodded. "Seriously, she does. She wore them last year when she won the National Junior Solo title."

"We put a little gold star sticker inside each of them—so we'd always know which ones were the Lucky Stars," Rochelle added.

"That's ridiculous," Liberty insisted. "You're going to miss your cue for a stupid pair of ballet shoes?"

"Here, honey." Scarlett's mom handed her another pair. "Just put these on. You'll be fine."

Scarlett raced to the wings just as the girl before her was taking her bows. It just didn't feel right without her lucky shoes! But she didn't have a choice. It was these or nothing. She flexed and pointed her toes, trying to will this pair to obey. She couldn't understand why her Lucky Stars had disappeared. She was sure she had tucked them into her dance bag after rehearsal. Maybe they'd fallen out?

"Next, we have a lyrical routine entitled 'In the Clouds,'" the announcer began.

"Wait! Wait!" Rochelle called. "Scarlett, I found them! They were under a bench in the hallway!"

She tossed the shoes to her friend, and Scarlett slipped them on just as her name was called: "Please welcome Scarlett from Dance Divas!"

Scarlett's heart was pounding as she stepped onto the stage. She felt the spotlight's warm glow as she took her position on the floor. She heard Miss Toni's words echo in her head as she danced: *"Straight legs . . . arms wide . . . head high, and shoulders down!"* She felt like a wave on the beach, ebbing and flowing with the swelling music, until suddenly, something went very wrong.

As Scarlett leaped and landed on the ball of her foot, she felt herself sliding across the stage.

There was a gasp from the audience as she came crashing down on the wood floor. She was facedown on the stage for what seemed like an eternity.

"Get up! Get up!" she heard Rock and Bria calling from the wings. So that's what she did. She pulled herself up and continued dancing from where she left off, struggling to keep with the music. The crowd cheered, but Scarlett could feel her cheeks burning. She was mortified. How could this have happened? She was so humiliated she could barely look the judges in the eye.

After the routine ended, she took a quick bow and raced offstage into her mom's arms. She burst into tears.

"It's okay, honey," her mom said, trying to comfort her. "Are you hurt?"

Scarlett touched her hip gingerly. It throbbed, and she was sure it was already turning black and blue. But her ego was bruised worse.

"I don't understand." She sobbed, looking at Rochelle and Bria. "It was going so well, then I just—"

"Wiped out." Miss Toni finished her sentence. "Let me see your ballet shoes."

On the bottom of the left slipper was a strange blue stain.

"What is that?" Scarlett sniffled.

Miss Toni rubbed her fingers across the sole. It felt slick and slippery. "If I had to guess, I'd say hair gel."

"How did hair gel get on your ballet shoe?" Bria asked.

"Maybe someone put it there," Liberty suddenly

said. "Let's see . . . *Who* was it that found your lucky shoes?" All eyes turned to Rochelle. Liberty pointed a finger in her face. "So much for best friends. Just sayin' . . ."

Rochelle suddenly remembered she had been using gel to do her bun moments before finding the shoes. "Oh my gosh! I'm so sorry, Scarlett! I might have had gel on my fingers! I didn't think— I just saw your shoes and tossed them out to you as fast as I could."

"It was an accident, Rock," Scarlett assured her. "You didn't mean to. It's okay."

Miss Toni clapped her hands. "Right now, we have a group number to do, and there'd better be no more mishaps. Clear?" Toni barked. "If there are, someone's head is going to be on the chopping block."

CHAPTER 8

The Tiny Terror

The competitive team from City Feet was up first in the Junior Small Group category. They marched through the halls backstage, chanting: "Move left! Move right! Move to the beat and make way for City Feet!" They were all dressed in silver sequin leotards and black tights studded with rhinestones.

"Big-time bling," Rochelle whispered in Scarlett's ear.

"Remember what I told you: game faces," Miss Toni warned the Divas as the girls marched by. "They can't scare us."

"Are you sure about that?" said a voice behind

them. It was Justine Chase. Scarlett recognized her from the photo.

"Justine . . . It's been ages," Toni answered with a forced smile.

"And you certainly look your age, Toni," Justine shot back. "Aww, is that a frown line I see? You should smile more! Then again, you were always so, so serious!"

Rochelle elbowed Scarlett in the ribs. "This is worse than we thought!" she whispered.

Toni took a deep breath. "And as I recall, you were always so, so sloppy, which I'm sure is still true."

"I wouldn't be so sure." Justine grinned. "Why don't you watch and find out?"

Just then, the announcer summoned the City Feet dancers to take their places.

"Pigs and crickets!" Justine called after them.

"Pigs and what?" Bria scratched her head.

"It means good luck." Toni groaned. "I do not like pigs and crickets—and I do not like Justine Chase." She went out to the audience to watch the performance unfold.

"*Phew.*" Rochelle whistled. "I'm glad she's mad at Justine and not me for a change!"

Scarlett peeked out from behind the curtain to catch a glimpse of Miss Toni. To say she looked angry was putting it mildly. She hadn't seen Toni this furious since Rochelle tossed her ballet shoes in the toilet and flooded the dressing room.

"I think Justine knows how to get under her skin," Scarlett said. It reminded her a lot of how Gracie knew exactly when and how to push her buttons. To be that good at bugging someone, you truly had to know her inside and out.

"You think they were enemies in ballet school, too?" Rochelle asked. "Maybe Mean Justine was a mean girl back then, too."

"She may be mean, but she's right. They look pretty fierce," Liberty said. She motioned to the five City Feet girls onstage. The lead dancer was a tiny girl—no more than Gracie's age—who took her position in a chin stand as the music began to play. She then exploded across the floor, tumbling and leaping in a breathless array of acrobatic moves. Their routine was called

"Hyperactive"—which pretty much described it perfectly. The number ended with a blast of fireworks and a spray of silver confetti on the audience.

"Sick! That is just sick!" Rochelle exclaimed.

"What is that gymnast—like five years old?" Liberty added.

Bria pulled out her phone and searched for City Feet again. "She's seven. Her name is Mandy Hammond . . . and her nickname is 'the Tiny Terror,'" she read. "She's been the National Petite champion three years in a row. Undefeated."

"Sick!" was all Rochelle could say again.

Scarlett watched as they dazzled the judges and the crowd. She could see Toni taking it all in from the back row. If she was as impressed as the Divas were, no one would be able to tell. She showed absolutely no emotion—not even when the crowd leaped to their feet in a standing ovation.

"We can't do that. We don't have anyone who can do that," Bria said, and sighed.

"I can do a better scissor leap!" Liberty insisted.

Rochelle glared. "You're not bad, but this girl has some serious acro moves. She's like an Olympic gymnast or something!"

Olympic gymnast? Scarlett suddenly thought of someone who might also be able to land many of those moves. She scanned the audience and found who she was looking for. There, front and center, was her little sister, Gracie, with their dad and grandparents. She was holding a bouquet of flowers on her lap, which Scarlett guessed were for her. Especially since Gracie was plucking the petals and tossing them on the floor, one by one.

"Gracie could do it," she said. "She's really good for her age. You should see her cartwheels."

"Gracie? As in your crazy little sister, Grace Face?" Liberty asked.

"She's not crazy! And if she is, well, you're not her sister, so you can't say that!" Scarlett exclaimed. The floor around Gracie's seat was now covered in red rose petals.

"But she's seven!" Liberty protested.

Bria shoved her phone in Liberty's face. "So is the Tiny Terror."

"There's no use talking about it now," Scarlett reminded them. "We're up next."

"Why bother?" Bria sighed. "They are so much better than we are."

"Do not let Toni hear you say that," Scarlett said. "We have to do this for her. We can't let City Feet win." They all agreed and placed their hands one on top of the other in the center of a huddle.

"One-two-three-four," chanted Scarlett.

"Dance Divas on the floor!" the other girls joined in.

"Five-six-seven-eight! Who's the team that's really great? DIVAS! DIVAS! Go, DANCE DIVAS!"

CHAPTER 9

And the Winner Is...

Scarlett knew the "Cyberbully" routine wasn't a typical dance-competition number. Her costume was a red beaded leotard and sheer tights splattered in red paint. The other girls wore black leotards with "thorny" branches wrapped around their bare arms. It was risky to say the least; "artsy" is what her mom had called it. But Scarlett could never have predicted the audience's reaction as the girls finished the routine. They carried her across the stage as the message "SIGNING OUT" flashed across the video screen behind them.

There was silence. Complete and utter silence.

When they returned for their bows, the judges were still staring at the stage, dumbstruck.

"This is either really good or really bad," Scarlett whispered to her teammates.

"That was so cool! Go, Scoot!" came a voice from the front row. *Thank goodness for Gracie!* Scarlett thought. The audience erupted in laughter, and the tension was broken. The crowd applauded enthusiastically, but Scarlett wasn't sure if it was for their dance or for Gracie's review.

Miss Toni waited in the wings, and as usual, her face was impossible to read. Had they messed up? Had they disappointed her? The girls braced themselves for her critique.

"I saw bent legs, girls, and Bria, you were a beat behind everyone else after the *tour jeté*." She paused. "But overall, good job." Then she walked back to the audience to wait for the award announcements.

"That's it?" asked Liberty.

"That's it," Scarlett replied. "It wasn't our best dance, but it wasn't our worst, either."

"I'd hate to see your worst," said a small voice from the wings.

"Oh no!" Bria whispered, ducking behind Scarlett. "It's the Tiny Terror!"

"Excuse me?" asked Scarlett. No seven-year-old was going to speak to her team that way.

"Nothing. I'm just saying I thought you guys would be serious competition. Our coach said so, but I guess she was wrong. I thought you were kind of lame."

"Listen up, pip-squeak," Liberty began. It was the first time Scarlett was actually glad to have Liberty on their side. "What's *lame* is the circus act you call a dance routine. I hear Ringling Brothers might have a few openings in the clown department."

Rochelle laughed out loud. "Good one, Lib!"

Mandy pursed her lips and narrowed her eyes. "Oh yeah?" she said.

The Divas stared her down. It was clear she had no comeback, so she stomped away.

"Wow, you sure put her in her place, Liberty," Scarlett said. "I didn't think you cared about the team."

"Of course, I do!" Liberty answered. "I mean . . . I guess."

Rochelle draped her arm around Liberty's shoulder. "I'm deeply touched," she teased. "Seriously, thanks for putting that little brat in her place. She has a bigger mouth than you."

"Oh no, she doesn't." Liberty smirked. "And you're welcome."

Scarlett's mom found the girls backstage. "Ladies," she said, "I hate to break up the fun, but they're about to announce the winners of the Junior Solos."

"Oh my gosh! That's me!" Liberty raced back onstage.

"And you," Rochelle said, and elbowed Scarlett.

"What's the use? I'm not going to win any medals, unless it's for best belly flop," Scarlett said, trying to make a joke, but her hip and her pride still hurt.

The announcer took the envelopes from the judges and cleared his throat. "Third place in the Junior Solo category . . . Scarlett Borden, 'In the Clouds,' from Dance Divas Studio!"

"You did it!" Rochelle hugged her.

"It's third place," Scarlett said with a sigh, "not first. Miss Toni always says 'It's first or nothing,' which makes me nothing." But she stood up, shook the announcer's hand, thanked the judges, and accepted her trophy.

"In second place, Phoebe Malone, 'Get on Your Feet,' City Feet Dance Studio!"

Scarlett grimaced. Miss Toni would not be happy that a City Feet girl had beaten her.

"And in first place in the Junior Solo category, Liberty Montgomery, 'Wings,' Dance Divas Studio!"

Liberty jumped to her feet and grabbed the trophy and tiara from the announcer.

"Way to go!" her mother shouted from the audience. Miss Toni was beaming as well.

"Next up . . . the winners for Junior Small Group," the announcer continued.

Bria grabbed Scarlett's and Rochelle's hands and squeezed them tight. "This is it!"

Scarlett hated the suspense. *At least let us place,* she thought.

"In third place, 'Sunny Side of the Street,' by Puttin' On the Ritz Dance Studio."

Scarlett's heart was beating so hard she could barely breathe. She didn't need to look out in the audience to know that Miss Toni was on the edge of her seat, too.

"Second place, Junior Small Group, goes to 'The Power of Love,' by Dance Elite!"

"That leaves just first place!" Bria exclaimed.

"We're toast." Rochelle sighed.

Scarlett noticed that Mandy was watching them. The entire City Feet team looked as cool as cucumbers. One girl was reapplying her lip gloss; another was texting on her phone.

"Finally, the top prize for Junior Small Group performance. First place goes to . . ."

A hush fell over the room. You could hear a bobby pin drop. Scarlett felt as if the world was standing completely still, waiting for their names to be plucked out of the envelope.

"City Feet Dance Studio for 'Hyperactive'!" the announcer's voice boomed through the ballroom.

The girls jumped to their feet and lifted Mandy high on their shoulders.

"Woo-hoo!" Mandy cheered. "We did it! We won!"

Scarlett applauded to show good sportsmanship, but inside she felt cold and empty. She actually shivered.

"We were robbed." Liberty fumed. "Our dance was way better than theirs. At least my part of it was."

"We lost. We have to face it," Scarlett said sadly. "And worse, we have to face Miss Toni."

CHAPTER 10
Sweet Revenge

Miss Toni sat in silence the entire bus ride back to New Jersey.

"She's scaring me," Rochelle remarked. "Why doesn't she say anything?"

"Maybe she's mad at us?" Bria suggested. "Maybe she's going to kick us all off the team?"

Scarlett shook her head. "No, I don't think she'd do that. I think she's just as devastated as we are."

Liberty was lying across the seat behind them, snuggling her poodle pillow. "Nope. I think she's planning her revenge against that rotten team. Which is what we should be doing instead of sitting here feeling sorry for ourselves."

"That's easy for you to say," Rochelle piped up. "You won first place in solos. You beat City Feet. Miss Toni is loving you."

Liberty smiled. "Everybody loves me."

"Not everybody," Rochelle muttered under her breath.

"Maybe Liberty is right," Scarlett said, considering the possibility. "I mean, what good is it feeling sorry for ourselves? We lost. What are we going to do about it?"

Liberty yawned. "Personally, I'm going to get some sleep."

Bria placed her head on Scarlett's shoulder. "Me, too."

Rochelle stretched out across a seat in front of them. "Me, three."

But Scarlett couldn't sleep a wink. Her mind was too busy going over the group number: every step, every turn, every detail. She thought that if she could just understand where they had gone wrong, it would make her feel better. She could close this chapter in the book and move forward. She drifted off to sleep, dreaming of the girls carrying her on their shoulders and feeling the sensation of floating weightlessly in the air.

"We're home, girls," her mom said, gently waking her as the bus pulled in front of the Dance Divas studio.

"What a day!" Mrs. Montgomery said. "Wait till I tell Madonna that Liberty won! She'll be so thrilled!"

Scarlett's and Bria's moms were less enthusiastic.

"I feel drained," Scarlett's mom said. "I'm glad it's over."

Scarlett looked into her dark-brown eyes. "Sorry, Mommy," she said. "I didn't mean to disappoint you."

"Disappoint me? You didn't disappoint me, honey!" she insisted. "You gave it your all. You know you can't win every competition." She swept a red curl out of Scarlett's eyes and tucked it behind her ear. "You have to let the other teams win a few trophies, right?"

"Not City Feet!" Rochelle said, gathering her bags. "That is one team I NEVER want to see win again."

"That is one team I never want to see again . . . period," Liberty said. "I've had enough of Mean Justine and her Tiny Terror."

Scarlett suspected Miss Toni felt the same. As they piled off the bus, Toni didn't say a word to the Divas or their moms. Not even good night.

Scarlett wasn't sure what to expect Monday afternoon in dance class. The last thing she saw coming was a giant candy bar!

"What in the world is *that*?" Liberty gasped as Miss Toni strolled into the studio carrying an enormous wooden chocolate-bar prop. She leaned it against the wall, dusted off her hands, and placed them on her hips.

"Does anyone know what this is?" she asked.

"Um, about a dozen cavities?" Rochelle joked.

"A huge bellyache?" Bria suggested.

"King Kong's snack?" Liberty threw out.

Toni shook her head. "No, no, and no. It's sweet revenge. Which is what we're going to get this weekend when we face City Feet again."

The girls looked at each other, confused, then at their dance teacher.

"We don't get it," Scarlett said, speaking for the team. "What's this weekend?"

"This weekend is the Feet on Fire dance competition in Hershey Park. I was able to get us in last minute, which means we're going head-to-head with your favorites again."

"Oh no!" Bria cried. "So soon?"

Miss Toni ignored the protests. "That gives us just five days to learn a new group routine, perfect it, and make the costumes. Warm up and be ready to go in five."

Scarlett wasn't sure what to think of the news. Part of her was terrified to lose again, but part of her really wanted the opportunity for Dance Divas to prove they were the best.

"I can't believe I have to see that pip-squeak Mandy standing on her head again!" Liberty said.

"Oh yeah." Rochelle remembered. "Mandy! We can't compete with those crazy acro moves. Who are we kidding?"

"Wait a sec," Scarlett said, racing out the studio door. Gracie was standing on a bench with her nose pressed against the studio window.

"Gracie, come here!" she called.

"Me? You want me to go in *there*?" her little sister asked. It was the first time Scarlett had ever invited her into a rehearsal space. Most of the time she had to sit outside, waiting for Scarlett's dance class to end so they could go home. "Won't Miss Toni be mad?"

"I think she's going to be really, really happy. Hurry up!"

She ushered Gracie inside the studio and instructed her to take off her shoes. Then she dragged over a padded mat and set it in front of the room.

"Scarlett," Miss Toni snapped. "You know I have rules about siblings staying outside . . ."

"Wait! Please! Just let her show you something!" Scarlett pleaded.

Miss Toni put down her clipboard. "Fine. You have one minute."

Scarlett turned to Gracie, who was staring wide-eyed at the dance coach. "I told you she'd be mad at me!" she said, and gulped. "Can I go now?"

"No!" Scarlett said. "We need your help! Please! Just show everyone your awesome cartwheels and side aerial."

Gracie shook her head. "But Miss Toni—"

Scarlett grabbed her sister by the shoulders. "Gracie, I am begging you! This is your chance to be a Dance Diva!"

Gracie nodded at her sister. Then she walked to one corner of the mat, took a deep breath, and dove into an impressive gymnastics floor routine. It was kind of wild but also kind of wonderful. Scarlett smiled—it was very Gracie.

"OMG!" Bria exclaimed. "She's good."

"She's great!" Scarlett said. "And with the right training—"

Miss Toni finished her thought: "We could have our own Tiny Terror." Then she turned to Gracie. "How would you like to be a Dance Diva?"

Gracie nodded her head and smiled. "Awesome!"

"You'll have to work hard . . . harder than you've ever worked before . . . and do absolutely everything I tell you. Clear?" Toni added.

The little girl clapped her hands and jumped up and down. "Yes! Yes! Oh my gooshness, I'm gonna be a Diva!"

"Then welcome to the team," Miss Toni said. "Take your place on the floor next to your sister, and let's get down to business."

Over the next few days, the Divas spent hours in the studio, learning the intricate choreography Miss Toni had created to crush their competition. She rolled in a TV on a table with a DVD player.

"Cool! Are we gonna watch a movie?" Gracie chirped.

"Is there popcorn?" Liberty asked.

Miss Toni clapped her hands. "Enough," she said. "This isn't movie night. We're going to study the competition. I want to show you why City Feet won last week—and why they're going to continue to win unless we do something about it."

She hit Play, and last week's dance routine popped onto the screen. "See how perfectly in sync they all are?" Toni pointed to the screen. "Phoebe has flawless technique—look at that intensity and confidence."

"I have intensity and confidence," Liberty piped up.

"You can say that again," Rochelle muttered.

"But you don't have that natural turnout," Toni pointed out. "Or that effortless *grand jeté*."

Scarlett had to admit: they were pretty amazing. Next to City Feet, Dance Divas looked like a big hot mess.

"Mandy is a powerhouse," Miss Toni continued. "She's young, but she goes for it, a hundred and ten percent." She looked over at Rochelle. "I don't see that from all of you."

After an hour of analyzing City Feet's performance, Miss Toni was pretty fired up.

"Everyone, on your feet!" she said.

Rochelle groaned. "It's going to be a long night. I can feel it."

They ran their routine over and over, trying to get the moves smooth and in sync. But that wasn't all. Thanks to the DVD, Miss Toni now wanted to see "projection."

"How do I project being a candy bar?" Rochelle complained.

"That should be easy for you . . . You're nuts!" Liberty smirked. "Get it? A candy bar with nuts?"

"Then clearly you should be a sour candy," Rochelle tossed back. "That's not a stretch."

"Guys, cool it. Miss Toni . . . ," Scarlett whispered.

But Miss Toni was way too busy picking apart the team's technique to pay attention to any squabbles between the girls. "I want to see razor-sharp kicks—no bent knees!" she screamed over the music. "Push! Push! Push!"

The number, "Sweet Revenge," was an acro dance filled with tricks and splits, set to a rapid-tempo disco tune. In the center of the stage would be Gracie, catapulting herself into a succession of flips. "Let me see that cartwheel," Miss Toni instructed her. "Now back handspring!"

"I can do a lot of them!" Gracie obliged, cart-wheeling across the entire studio floor.

"Not bad, not bad," her coach replied. "But, Gracie, you have to control your energy and your movements. You have to focus them so they're precise and contained. Got it?"

Scarlett chuckled. If Toni thought she could control Gracie's energy, good luck! Her mom always said that trying to make Gracie sit still was like try-ing to hold a wet bar of soap in your hands. It always slipped out from between your fingers.

"Do you think we'll win this weekend?" Gracie asked Scarlett.

Honestly, Scarlett didn't know. City Feet was a force to be reckoned with, and she wasn't quite sure the Divas were ready to take them on again.

"We'll try our hardest," she told Gracie. She was relieved that Gracie was acting like a team player who wanted to help Dance Divas—not just skip off and play with her Barbies.

"Good." Gracie smiled. " 'Cause I really want to win a big trophy. Or a crown. A crown would be so cool! I'd wear it all the time!"

Okay, maybe Gracie had some ulterior motives. But Scarlett suspected Miss Toni did as well. She knew that this weekend's competition wasn't just about beating City Feet. It was about beating Justine.

CHAPTER 11

Candy Couture

Beating City Feet wasn't the only thing the Divas had to worry about. Miss Toni instructed each of them to decorate a costume with real candy: Kisses, gummy bears, licorice, anything that could be stitched or hot-glued on to give their outfits "sweet appeal."

Gracie was excited. She loved a craft project. "Yum!" she said, pouring bags of treats on the floor of their living room. Her mom had found Halloween candy on sale at the supermarket. "What about gummy worms? Or these?" She held up a black licorice spider.

"*Ew*, no way!" Scarlett said, picking through mounds of gummy eyeballs and candy corn. "Miss Toni said bright and pretty. Gummy brains are not bright and pretty."

"But they taste good," Gracie said, popping a few in her mouth.

"Honey, don't eat all the embellishments," her mother said, and sighed. "I'm going to need a lot to cover these leotards. And you'll give yourself a bellyache."

It took several hours of trial and error to figure out how to get the candies to stick. Scarlett's mom decided a hot-glue gun was the answer.

"It stays on, but it also melts the candy." Scarlett sighed. "These jelly beans are jelly goo!"

"Maybe Toni won't notice," her mom said hopefully.

"Miss Toni notices everything," Gracie said, popping a handful of Swedish fish in her mouth. "Do we have any more of these?"

Scarlett agreed. It was hard to pull one over on their dance coach. But desperate times called for desperate measures. They had only two days before the competition, and they had to make something sweet and suitable to wear onstage.

At the studio the next afternoon, Miss Toni asked all the girls to line up in the back of the room. "I want each of you to walk, one by one, modeling your candy couture."

"I feel like I'm on *Project Runway*," Bria said. "This is really nerve-racking!"

Gracie rubbed her stomach. "My tummy still hurts from yesterday," she said with a moan.

"No one told you to eat a pound of gummy brains," Scarlett scolded her.

Liberty rolled her eyes. "I seriously do not want to know what that means."

"Bria, you're first!" Toni called.

"Work it!" Rochelle said, giving her teammate a push. Bria tried her best to stroll across the floor with confidence. But she felt pretty ridiculous in her yellow leotard covered in Sour Patch Kids.

"It's bright," Miss Toni said, motioning for her to turn around. "But what happened here? Where are the candies?" She pointed to an empty patch on Bria's shoulder.

Bria looked embarrassed. "I ate them while I was studying in the dressing room. Sorry. Tests make me stressed!"

Rochelle was up next. She strutted like a super-model, swinging her hips and arms as she modeled her brown velvet unitard covered in mini chocolate bars.

"What's that?" Toni pointed to a strange muddy trail along the studio floor.

"I think I'm melting," Rochelle replied. "I guess when you're as hot as I am, the chocolate gets mushy?" Miss Toni did not look at all amused.

Scarlett raised her hand. "Um, I have a similar problem," she began. "When these Sugar Daddy candies melt, it's like Super Glue! I think my ballet shoe is stuck to the floor!"

"Anyone have strawberries?" Liberty joked. "I love fondue!"

"That's enough!" Toni barked. Things were not going as she had planned. "What is that on *your* costume?" she asked Liberty. Her pink leotard looked like it had been sprinkled with fairy dust.

"It's Pucker Powder—check it out!" She spun gracefully in a *pirouette*.

"*Achoo!*" Gracie suddenly sneezed. "The powder tickles my nose!"

Miss Toni sunk down on her stool and shook her head. "This is a disaster!"

"A fashion disaster—the worst kind," Liberty said.

"I'm afraid she's gonna go ballistic and eat us!" Rochelle added.

Gracie looked terrified. "Like the witch in 'Hansel and Gretel'? What should we do, Scoot?"

Scarlett stood perfectly still, waiting for Miss Toni's verdict on the candy costume catastrophe. "Don't ask me. I couldn't run if I wanted to." She tried to pull her ballet shoe up off the floor, but it had a sticky glob of caramel attached to it.

"I want everyone to start over from scratch," Toni finally announced. "No candy that melts, drips—"

"Or makes me sneeze!" Gracie piped up.

"Precisely," Toni replied. "I know we have very little time, but I want every outfit to be clean, bright, beautiful, and dance ready." She turned to Bria. "And no snacking on your costume till *after* the competition. Clear?"

Bria nodded and remained silent. She had a Sour Patch Kid in her mouth.

Once the girls had changed and cleaned up, Miss Toni pulled the giant wooden chocolate bar out of the closet again.

"I was wondering what happened to that thing," Liberty said.

"Ladies, I have come up with a finale for our dance that is going to make the judges' mouths water." Toni dragged the prop into the middle of the room.

"I want the four of you to lift this candy bar high in the air, as high as you can. And Gracie, I want you to do a backbend on top."

Gracie crinkled her nose. "On top of there? In the air?"

Scarlett raised her hand. "Miss Toni, Gracie is a little scared of heights."

"Am not!" Gracie insisted.

"Gracie, remember the Ferris wheel at the state fair last summer? Remember how you screamed, 'Get me down from here'?" (Scarlett kindly left out the part where Gracie threw up.)

Gracie's cheeks flushed. Scarlett didn't want to embarrass her, but she knew there was no way her little sis could do this stunt.

"I can do it! Let me try!" Gracie pushed past Scarlett and climbed onto the chocolate bar.

"Arch your back, keep your hands and feet planted firmly," Toni instructed her. "Do not wobble or you will fall. Clear?"

Gracie gulped. "Yeah."

"Liberty and Bria, you are in the front; Rochelle and Scarlett in the back. When I say 'lift,' lift."

Gracie stood tall with her arms above her head as the girls heaved the chocolate bar high in the air above their heads.

"I'm a little dizzy," Gracie whispered to Scarlett. "It's so high!"

"Close your eyes!" Scarlett told her. "Don't think about it. Just imagine the cool Dance Diva jacket you get to wear on Saturday."

"I do?" Gracie asked. "My own?"

"Yup," Rochelle chimed in. "All blinged out and beautiful!" She winked at Scarlett.

Gracie lifted her arms over her head, pushed her hips forward, then reached for the ground, keeping her arms by her ears, just as Miss Toni had shown her.

"Perfect backbend!" Miss Toni applauded. "Do it like that on Saturday, and we're going to be the team to beat."

That's what I'm afraid of, Scarlett thought. Being beaten again by City Feet would be beyond humiliating. It could even mean the end of the Dance Divas' competition season.

CHAPTER 12

I Spy

"Look at all those awesome rides!" Gracie gushed as they pulled into Hershey Park. "Oooh! I can smell chocolate. Can you smell it, Scoot? Can we go on the rides? Please, Scoot? Pretty please?"

Scarlett didn't know why she agreed to sit next to Gracie the entire three-hour ride to Hershey Park. Maybe it was because she gave her those big brown, puppy-dog eyes.

"Don't you want to sit with Mom?" Scarlett suggested.

"No! I want to sit with the team," she insisted. "I'm a Diva. Oh yeah!"

She sang her own made-up tunes for the first forty-five minutes, then insisted on playing a game of Uno. At one point, the bus came to a quick stop, and the cards went flying everywhere.

"Cool!" Gracie giggled, tossing the rest of the deck in the air.

"Really?" Liberty complained, picking a draw 4 card out of her lap. "Your little sis is a lot of fun, *Scoot*."

Scarlett was relieved when they finally got off the bus and she could focus on the competition. Gracie was too busy shaking hands with a giant Reese's Peanut Butter Cup character to bug her. Once they checked into the Hotel Hershey, there was barely any time to unpack before Toni scheduled a rehearsal.

"But I wanna go on the chocolate factory tour!" Gracie moped. "Why do we always have to rehearse? It's so boring!"

"Gracie, you wanted to be part of the team," her mom explained. "That means being a team player. You do what everyone else does."

"Besides," Scarlett pointed out, "the competition is over tonight. We can go on the factory tour tomorrow morning."

"Promise?" Gracie pouted. "I want to buy one of those jumbo chocolate Kisses. I'm gonna eat the whole thing."

"I'm sure you will!" Her mom laughed. "Maybe you can save me *one* bite?"

Gracie smiled. "Well, maybe one. And one for you, too, Scoot."

"Thanks," Scarlett said. But chocolate was the last thing on her mind. All she could think of was winning.

"Let's go practice, Gracie," she said, taking her sister by the hand. "Don't forget your Dance Divas jacket!"

"Oh yeah!" Gracie said, pulling on the black satin jacket and admiring the gold logo on the back in a mirror. "I look cooooool!"

"The coolest!" Scarlett said. "Now hurry . . . please!"

When they arrived for rehearsal, Bria, Liberty, and Rochelle were already there, with their ears pressed against the meeting-room wall.

"What are you guys doing?" Scarlett asked.

"What does it look like we're doing?" said Liberty, hushing her. "We're eavesdropping on the competition. Those City Feet freaks are rehearsing, too."

"Their music is really slow and soft. Sounds like lyrical to me," Rochelle said.

"Let me hear!" Gracie said, pushing in between them. "What are they saying?"

"Something about 'bag' and 'over'?" Bria said, straining to make out the words.

Miss Toni walked into the room. "Vaganova. It's a Russian ballet technique. What are you girls up to?"

"City Feet is next door, and we're spying on them!" Gracie volunteered.

"No, you are not." Toni sniffed. "Because that is bad sportsmanship."

"But if we knew that they were planning, we could make our routine better than theirs,"

Rochelle said. "Why shouldn't we do everything we can to win?"

"Because we're Divas. And we're going to win this competition on our own merits. Not by knowing someone else's routine. So step away from the wall and hit the floor. Now."

Scarlett knew Miss Toni was right. But she still wished she knew what the City Feet team was planning for their group number. Was it contemporary? Jazz? Lyrical? What did their costumes look like?

"I have an idea how we can find out what they're planning," Liberty whispered to Scarlett. "Are you with me?"

She nodded.

"Then bring Grace Face and meet me outside in five."

Liberty raised her hand to get Miss Toni's attention. "I forgot my jazz shoes upstairs. Sorry! Be right back!" she said, dashing out the door.

Miss Toni rolled her eyes. "All right, unless there are any other interruptions, I want to take it from the top—"

"Gracie needs to go to the bathroom. I'll take her," said Scarlett.

"No, I don't—" Gracie started to say, but Scarlett covered her mouth with her hand. "Now, Gracie, what did Mom say about holding it in for too long? We don't want a puddle on the floor, do we?" She dragged her little sister into the hall, winking.

"I don't have to go!" Gracie screamed once they were outside.

"I know! But don't you want to help Liberty and me on a top-secret spy mission?"

"Really?" Gracie beamed. "Cool!"

Liberty was already waiting for them at the door to City Feet's meeting room. "Okay, Gracie. Here's the plan. You go on in the room and pretend you made a mistake. Say, 'Sorry! I thought this was my room.' They don't know you're with us yet. They'll just think you're a little kid who got lost. Take a good look around and report back everything you see and hear. Got it?"

Gracie nodded. "Got it!"

Scarlett and Liberty crossed their fingers as Gracie slowly opened the door. The dancers were all gathered in a circle around a girl in *pointe* shoes. They were wrapping her in a long white scarf, swaying back and forth as she twirled in the center.

"Excuse me?" Justine said, spotting Gracie. "Are you looking for someone?"

"Yes! I mean, no!" Gracie replied. "I, um, I got lost. I'm not supposed to be here. Bye!"

She ran out of the room and down the hall to where Liberty and Scarlett were waiting.

"Okay . . . what did you see?" Liberty demanded.

"Ghosts!" Gracie panted. "Spooky ghosts."

Scarlett groaned. "Come on, Gracie. Stop joking around. What were they doing?"

"I'm not making it up! There were ghosts all around this one ballerina. She was really, really good."

"So they were doing a ballet routine about ghosts?" Liberty asked. "This makes no sense!"

"You're sure, Gracie?" Scarlett asked her.

"Cross my heart!" she said. "I saw ghosts."

During their break, they shared what they learned with Rochelle and Bria.

"Okay, let me search for it: a ghost ballet," Bria said, typing fast and furiously on her phone's keyboard. "I got it! I got it! They're doing *Giselle*!"

She showed the girls a video from a website of a beautiful ballerina, dressed all in white, dancing eerily on a grave.

"*Eww*, that is really creepy," Rochelle said, and shuddered.

"That's it." Gracie nodded. "That's what she looked like."

"It's classic ballet. It didn't seem like ballet was their thing," said Liberty.

"How many girls were there?" Rochelle asked Gracie.

"Um, well, five in the circle, and the ballerina in the middle."

"There were only five girls last week," Bria said, "and there are only five names listed on their elite-team website. Who's the ballerina in the middle?"

Scarlett shook her head. "It's worse than we thought. They have a secret weapon!"

CHAPTER 13

Time to Shine

"So you're saying that City Feet has a new dancer?" Rochelle asked.

"Well, she wasn't there last week, was she?" Liberty replied. "I wonder what they're up to."

"We're not going to find out standing around here," Scarlett said. "But I bet I know someone who might blab all the details."

"Who?" Bria asked.

Liberty, Rochelle, and Scarlett all answered at once: "Mandy!"

It wasn't difficult to find Mandy roaming the halls of the hotel. They waited until her mom went into the gift shop to corner her.

"Hi ya, Mandy," Liberty said.

"What do you want?" Mandy asked, unshaken.

"I just wanted to tell you that we're going to kick your butts tonight," Liberty said.

"Oh yeah? In your dreams!" Mandy shot back.

"We know all about the ballerina . . . and the ghosts," Scarlett added.

"How did you find out?" Mandy gasped. "That's a secret! No one is supposed to know about Anya!"

Scarlett looked at Liberty and shrugged. "Well, we know all about her," Liberty improvised. "You're not as smart as you think you are!"

Mandy shrieked, "I am so telling Miss Justine on you guys! And Mr. and Mrs. Bazarov!" She stamped off in a huff.

Bria began searching the name Anya Bazarov immediately. "All I can find is something about her competing in Los Angeles last year. She was a member of the Shooting Starz Studio team," she reported.

"How did she do?" Scarlett asked.

Bria swallowed hard. "First overall in the Teen

Solos twice. She seems like a pretty serious bal-lerina."

"That's it. We're toast again!" Rochelle sighed. "Now we have Anya Bizarre-o to worry about, too."

"Wait! It says she competed in the Teen division—which is twelve and up," Bria said, scan-ning the article. "And that was last year. So how is she dancing as a *Junior* with them? In Juniors, you can't be older than eleven."

"Bria, you're a genius!" Scarlett hugged her. "She's too old. City Feet must be lying about her age."

They ran to find Toni to tell her what they'd discovered.

"I told you girls, no spying on the competi-tion!" she scolded.

"But Miss Toni," Scarlett pleaded. "Anya is doing a *Junior* Solo and she's thirteen. They're cheating."

"And so are you . . . by sticking your nose where it doesn't belong. I'm surprised at you, Scarlett. I expect more of you."

Toni turned to face the rest of the team. "I don't want to hear another word about this. Change into your costumes, get out there, and dance your best. Stop worrying about other teams and worry about yourselves."

She stormed off in a huff. Scarlett felt terrible. Miss Toni had never spoken to her that way before. She felt like she'd let Miss Toni down—and all she was trying to do was help.

In the dressing room, Scarlett found her mom sewing lollipops last-minute onto Gracie's costume.

"Miss Toni is mad at me," she told her.

"We heard—Gracie told us what happened. Spying on them wasn't right," her mother said.

"But we found out some really important stuff. Stuff that could disqualify their team from the competition."

Her mother looked up from her work. "And that's what you want? To win because they had to forfeit? That doesn't sound like a very satisfying win to me."

Scarlett hated when her mother was right. It made her feel guilty.

But there was nothing to be done about it now. The group dances were starting, and City Feet was up first.

Bria was correct: their number was a modern take on *Giselle*. The girls were all ghosts dancing in a cemetery. Anya Bazarov was everything the article said: a "beautifully poised ballerina." And Mandy was every bit as impressive as she had been at City Lights. Only now her face was painted a ghostly white and her hair was sprinkled with baby powder.

"They really deserve to win first place, don't they?" Rochelle asked Scarlett. "That Bizarre-o girl is *gooood*."

"Probably. But we're going to give them a run for it."

When it was the Divas' turn, the girls strutted out to center stage in their brightly colored costumes covered in real candy. Liberty was pink bubble gum, Rochelle was blue starlight mints,

Bria was green gumballs, and Scarlett was red licorice. Gracie was the cutest of all: a rainbow-swirled lollipop. This time nothing melted or fell off (thanks to a ton of Super Glue!), and the number was light and fun and showed off little Gracie's tumbling. Every time she did a cartwheel, her face lit up, and the judges seemed delighted. She didn't even wobble as the girls lifted her high in the air.

"That was flawless!" Liberty's mom told them as they exited the stage. "Not a step out of place."

"I saw a few," Miss Toni said. "But good job, ladies. Really good job."

At least, Scarlett thought, their coach was proud of their performance. Maybe she'd let the whole spying incident slip? Nonetheless, she felt like there was something she still had to do. She saw Mandy walking back to her dressing room and stopped her.

"I just wanted to say I'm sorry," she told Mandy. "What we did to you . . . it was wrong. It was mean."

Mandy stared. She wasn't expecting an apology. "Why did you do it?" she asked.

"I guess because we were afraid you were going to beat us again."

Mandy smirked. "We *are* going to beat you."

Scarlett nodded. "Then you'll beat us fair and square. No tricks. My mom always says a win when you cheat doesn't feel like a win at all."

As she walked away, Scarlett saw Miss Toni standing at the end of the hall. That was all she needed: another lecture about talking to the competing team and sticking her nose where it didn't belong. She braced herself.

"I'm proud of you," Miss Toni said instead. "I was eavesdropping. Some girls I know taught me how."

"I'm not sure Mandy really cared what I had to say," Scarlett told her. "But at least I apologized."

Toni nodded. "I know it's hard to do the right thing when you want something so badly. But when you do the wrong thing, you have to live with yourself."

Scarlett wasn't exactly sure what Toni was talking about. It sounded personal. Had she made a mistake in the past? Done something wrong that she now regretted? At least she knew her teacher wasn't furious with her—or planning to cut her from the team.

"They're about to announce the winners. You'd better get out there," Toni said. The stage was already packed with contestants eager to hear the results.

When it came time to announce the group awards, the emcee held up his hand and asked for everyone's attention.

"Judges, we have a protest regarding a contestant's age."

Liberty looked at Scarlett. "You don't think Toni went to the judges, do you?"

Scarlett couldn't imagine it—not after her lecture about minding your own business. But when she saw Justine and Anya standing before the judges' table with a stack of papers, she realized it was a definite possibility.

They debated for a while before handing down a verdict: Anya had lied about her age. She was thirteen—which put her in the Teen division. And because she had exhibited "unsportsmanlike behavior" by fudging her paperwork, she would be disqualified from her solo. To be fair, points would also be deducted from City Feet's group number.

"Take that, City Feet!" Liberty cheered. "That'll show you not to mess with the Divas."

"Zip it!" Rochelle hushed her. "They're announcing the top three groups."

The third and second spots went to Toes and Bows from Connecticut and InSync Dance from Staten Island.

Scarlett took a deep breath and waited for the announcer to open the last envelope. "Well, no surprise here," he ad-libbed. "This group had some *sweet* moves today! Congratulations to . . . the Dance Divas Studio!"

Scarlett wasn't sure who was screaming the loudest, Liberty or Gracie. "We won! We won!"

They held hands and jumped up and down. The girls all rushed toward the announcer to collect their trophy and pose for pictures. As the flashes popped, Scarlett couldn't stop smiling. It felt amazing to be back on top.

Then she saw Justine walking toward them.

"Congrats, Toni," she said, extending a hand for her to shake. "I guess I underestimated your team."

"They're good girls," Toni replied. She kept her hands firmly in her pockets.

"There's no rule against recruiting a gifted young dancer from L.A.," Justine said.

"No, but there is a rule about faking your age on an application. She's a gifted *thirteen-year-old* dancer—which makes her a Teen, not a Junior."

"And you just had to go and blab to the judges, didn't you?" Justine asked.

"I didn't tell anyone," Toni said calmly.

"I did," said a small voice. It was Mandy.

Scarlett gasped. As much as she didn't like Mandy, she wanted to run up to her at this moment and hug her!

"But why?" Justine demanded. "Why would you do that to your team?"

Mandy repeated what Scarlett had told her: "Because a win when you cheat doesn't feel like a win at all."

Justine looked Toni in the eyes. "I didn't know Anya lied about her age," she said.

Toni raised an eyebrow. "You sure about that? As I recall from our ABC days, lies were your specialty."

"Are you ever going to get over it?" Justine sighed. "It's been twenty years."

Toni shook her head. "Some things you never forget . . . like a best friend who stabs you in the back."

CHAPTER 14

Ancient History

All week long after the Feet on Fire win, Scarlett kept playing the Toni-Justine conversation over and over in her head.

"She said they were best friends," she told Rochelle while they were getting ready for stretch class. "Like how we're best friends. How weird is that?"

"Really weird. I didn't think Toni had any friends," Rochelle said, and giggled.

"Justine must have done something really awful for Miss Toni to hate her so much," Scarlett continued. "I wonder what it was."

"Can I just remind you about the no-spying policy Miss Toni made us all swear to," Bria piped up. "I'm all for cyberdetective work, but I'm scared. Miss Toni said 'Mind your own beeswax' and she meant it."

"She meant it about the City Feet team," Liberty pointed out. "This isn't about them. It's about Miss Toni."

"And Justine," Rochelle said. "But I guess they weren't coaches when this all happened, right?"

"Right!" Scarlett typed in the website for American Ballet Company on Bria's laptop and clicked on the tab marked "School Archives." She scanned through about a dozen pictures, searching for photos of Toni's performances as a young ballerina.

"Aha!" she exclaimed, when she came across a group photo. There, dressed in red fire-bird costumes, were Toni and Justine. Another picture showed them dancing side by side in the *corps de ballet* of *Coppélia*.

"They were always in the front row together," Bria noted.

"Until this year," Scarlett said. "Look at all these photos of Justine." She was Odette in *Swan Lake*, Juliet dancing with her Romeo, Cinderella at the ball.

"No Toni?" Rochelle asked. "That's weird."

"That's the key," Scarlett said.

"Do you seriously think this whole Toni-Justine feud is about Toni losing out on leads in ballet school?"

"I know how to find out," Liberty said. She clicked on the tab marked "Alumni" and found Justine's e-mail.

"What are you going to say?" Scarlett asked, worried. "Miss Toni is going to freak if she finds out you're e-mailing Justine."

"She won't find out," Liberty insisted. "I'll create a fake e-mail account."

Then she typed, "Meet me in the lobby of the Atlantic City Convention Center before Nationals—Toni." She hit Send before the rest of the girls had a chance to chicken out.

"It might fix things between them," Bria said hopefully.

"Or it might start World War Three!" Scarlett sighed. Nationals was three months away, and both City Feet and Dance Divas would be competing. Maybe Justine would be way too busy with her team to meet Toni. Maybe she wouldn't even want to.

Bria's laptop suddenly dinged. There was an e-mail.

"See you there. Justine."

CHAPTER 15

A Little Bit of Luck

The National Reach for the Stars dance competition in Atlantic City, New Jersey, was never something Miss Toni took lightly. But this year she posted the date three months ahead of time on a huge hot-pink poster on the wall and outlined a schedule of rehearsals, costume fittings, and private lessons that made Scarlett's head spin. To compete, a team needed to place first in at least one regional competition. Which made both Dance Divas *and* City Feet eligible.

"This is in our home state—so it's even more important that we sweep every category," Toni began. "People from all over are going to be coming to watch us. Do not embarrass me. But most important, don't embarrass yourselves."

She posted a list of solos, duos, trios, and three group routines. "You'll learn all of these, and I'll decide which ones are good enough to enter," she continued. "I thought we'd try out a few of the dances this weekend at the Dance Divas Studio showcase."

She turned to Gracie. "You're getting your very own solo called 'Watch Out, World—Here I Come!'"

Scarlett expected her sister to jump for joy. Instead, she looked like she was going to be sick.

"What's wrong, Gracie?" she whispered.

"A solo means you have to be onstage all by yourself. What if I mess up? Everyone will see!"

"You have nothing to worry about," Scarlett promised her. "We'll all be in the audience."

"I know. Not on the stage!" Gracie whined. "I like group numbers, not solos."

The more Scarlett tried to calm her down, the

more nervous Gracie got. By Saturday morning's recital, she was a bundle of nerves.

"You look so cute!" her mom said, adjusting the bow tie around her neck. It was Toni's idea to have her wear a black velvet leotard that looked like a tux. Even Scarlett had to admit she looked downright adorable in her pigtails and black fishnet stockings.

"Just remember not to rush the back walk-over," Scarlett reminded her. "And tuck your head when you do your rolls. Don't pop it up like a turtle."

Scarlett heard Miss Toni introducing her dance once, twice, then a third time. "Go on!" Scarlett whispered, giving her sister a little shove. Gracie slowly walked to the center of the stage. She looked out at the audience, filled with faces she recognized: her parents, her grandparents, and her friends from school, gymnastics, and the dance studio. There were also dozens of strangers—and *everyone* was looking at her. She stood frozen.

"Oh no . . . she has stage fright!" Bria said. "You have to do something, Scarlett. You're her big sis."

Scarlett remembered how Gracie's cheers of "Go, Scoot!" after the disastrous "Cyberbully" number had made her feel better. "Go, Gracie!" she yelled from the wings. "You can do it!" The rest of the team joined in: "Go, Gracie! Go, Gracie!" and the audience began to clap.

But Gracie's feet remained stuck to the stage. She didn't do a handspring or a cartwheel or even a somersault. Instead, she slowly backed away from the front of the stage. Then she turned and made a run for it.

Toni dropped the curtain, and Scarlett caught Gracie in her arms. She was crying just like the time her favorite Barbie broke.

"Gracie, it's okay." Scarlett tried to comfort her. "You just got a little scared. It's your first solo."

Gracie shook her head. "No, I can't do it by myself," she said, sobbing. "I don't want to."

"Great. We have a Tiny Terror who's terrified of being onstage by herself," Liberty complained. "That's a big help."

"Leave her alone." Scarlett defended her sister. There had been several times in the past when she had wanted to make a run for it, too—including the time she slipped onstage. "Gracie, we all get scared sometimes. But the more you dance, the more confident you get."

Gracie wiped her runny nose on the back of her hand. "You think so?"

"I know so!" Scarlett said.

"Uh-oh," Rochelle said. She'd spotted Miss Toni making a beeline for their group. Scarlett knew how Toni reacted when someone left the stage without completing her dance routine. It made her see red. She hoped Gracie wasn't in for one of her lectures.

"Gracie?" Toni asked. "What happened out there?"

Gracie's face was streaked with tears. "I got scared. I couldn't remember the routine."

Toni nodded. "That happens to even the best dancers sometimes. But you have to take a deep breath and focus. You have to fight your nerves. Clear?"

Gracie nodded her head, and, thankfully, Toni

went back to the rest of the showcase. Though she hated how Gracie always got special treatment because she was younger, this was one time Scarlett was happy to see her get off easy.

Gracie, however, didn't feel that way. "I'll never be a Diva now," she said with a sniffle.

"Of course you will," Scarlett promised her.

She tried to think of what calmed her down before a performance. Everyone had a little ritual: Bria crossed her fingers and toes; Rochelle said the alphabet backward. Liberty kissed her reflection in the mirror. And she . . .

"Gracie, I think I know something that will help—stay here." Scarlett ran back to the dressing room and took a sheet of tiny gold stickers out of her bag. They were the same ones she'd used to mark her Lucky Star ballet shoes.

"Gracie," she said. "I hereby present you with my lucky stars."

Gracie looked at the gold foil stars her sister was holding. "They're just stickers."

"No, they're a lot more than that. If you put

them in your shoes and make a wish, your wish will come true."

Gracie wrinkled her nose. She wasn't sure if Scarlett was pulling her leg.

Rochelle vouched for her. "It's true. They're Scarlett's lucky charms."

"You mean like 'Star light, star bright . . . / Wish I may, wish I might'?" she asked.

"Exactly!" Scarlett answered. "Give me your shoe, and I'll show you." She peeled off a star and placed it inside the back heel. "Whenever you dance, you'll know you have some extra star power on your side."

Gracie nodded, then she hugged her big sister tight. "Love you to the moon, Scoot."

Scarlett smiled back. "Love you to the stars!"

CHAPTER 16

The Big Day

Three months of rehearsals flew by, and the day of the Reach for the Stars competition completely sneaked up on Scarlett.

"I can't believe it's tomorrow," she told Rochelle. "I'm not sure we're ready."

"I'm ready," Liberty said. "Wait till you see my costume! The designer for Katy Perry made it."

"And wait till you see mine." Rochelle imitated Liberty, tossing her hair and sashaying around the dressing room. "The designer for Rochelle Hayes made it . . . my mom!"

Scarlett tried not to laugh. "Come on, guys.

I'm sure all the costumes are great. I just wish Toni would make up her mind which soloists she's choosing."

"I hope it's not me." Bria sighed. "My social studies teacher announced a test for Monday. I have to memorize all the constitutional amendments, and I don't know any of them!"

"How many are there?" Gracie asked.

Bria frantically flipped through her textbook. "I don't even know! Ten? Thirteen? Twenty-five? It might as well be a million! I'm going to fail anyway."

"Don't worry. We'll help you study, Bria," Scarlett said, putting an arm around her friend.

"When? Between rehearsals? Before costume fittings? At the competition? There's just no time!" Bria looked more panicked than Scarlett had ever seen her.

"You know, studying is a lot like learning a dance combination," Scarlett told her. "You have to just go over it and over it till you nail it."

Bria shook her head. "No, it's different. When

I dance, I have the music to remind me what comes next."

"Then put some beats to it!" Rochelle said, taking the textbook from her. "This is my specialty!"

She began to rap: "The First Amendment says you're free, to say anything you like to me—"

"Really?" Liberty smirked. "*Anything?* Can I say that your beatboxing is sad and amateurish?"

Scarlett scowled. "Liberty, let's not distract Bria. The point Rock was trying to make was that studying can be fun and easy."

"Maybe for you," Bria said, pouting. "Not for me."

"Could you at least give it a shot?" Rochelle asked. "Here." She handed Bria back her book and her notes.

Bria looked them over, closed her eyes, and rapped: "Amendment Four—that's no bore. It says you better stay out of my door!"

"That's right!" Scarlett cheered. "It's 'no search or seizure without a warrant'! Bria, you nailed it!"

"Two down, twenty-five more to go!" Bria said, then moaned.

"But you know you can do this," Scarlett insisted. "Just put it to a beat and start moving your feet."

Suddenly Toni burst into the dressing room. "I'd like you all to start moving your feet—into the studio this minute. I have decided the final lineup for Nationals." She handed them each a sheet of paper listing the numbers and who would be dancing them.

"Yes! I have a solo!" Liberty pumped her fist in the air.

Scarlett scanned the list for her name and saw it under a trio with Rochelle and Bria. The only other solo was Gracie in the Petite category.

"I don't get it," she said. "I always solo at Nationals."

"You mean you always *used* to solo," Liberty corrected her. "Miss Toni obviously has a new favorite dancer in the house."

"Cut it out, Liberty," Rochelle warned her. "This isn't a contest to win the teacher's-pet title."

"It isn't?" Liberty asked innocently. "Gee, maybe that's because none of you are winning? Just saying . . ."

Scarlett hated to admit it, but Liberty had a point. Miss Toni had never quite forgiven her for the slipup at Feet on Fire, and Toni's word was final. Liberty and Gracie were the soloists.

She was glad to be dancing with Bria and Rock, though. Their trio was a spicy contemporary dance called "House of Cards." Each of them was dressed like a suit in the deck: Bria was clubs, Rochelle was hearts, and she was diamonds.

The group number was equally exciting. Miss Toni called it "The Untouchables," and the girls played old-time gangsters robbing a bank. The music sounded like a tense staccato piano from a silent movie, and their costumes were all black, white, and silver. In the end, Gracie—the long arm of the law—arrested the bad guys (her little sis loved that part!) and rescued the loot.

"TTFN—that means ta-ta for now!" Liberty said. "I'm off to a private session with Miss Toni to run my solo."

"TTFW—that means too tacky for words," Rochelle called after her, "which is how I'm sure you'll dance tomorrow onstage!"

The Convention Center in Atlantic City was one of the biggest venues at which the Divas had ever performed.

"It says the competition is in Exhibit Hall D, and our rehearsal room is off Hall C," Bria said as she read the floor plans.

"It's so big!" Gracie looked at the giant windows and sky-high ceilings.

"Let's get a look at the space," Miss Toni said, ushering them into the main exhibit hall. None of the girls had ever seen anything like it: there was bleacher-style seating—enough for thousands of people—and a stage the size of a small football field.

"This is crazy!" Scarlett exclaimed.

"Totally!" Liberty added. "I'm going to look like a flea to the people sitting in the back row."

"I told you all this was a huge venue," Toni said. "Bigger than any of the other Nationals we've competed in. I hope it's sinking in now."

Rochelle nodded. "I feel like a rock star."

"Good," Toni replied. "Just perform like one today."

The girls spent the morning running through their complicated choreography. Thankfully, Miss Toni didn't switch things up. "I want to spend the last hour working on the solos," she told Liberty and Gracie. "The rest of you, take five."

They decided to stroll around the lobby, scouting out the competition as it rolled in on buses from around the country. Bria spotted some of their old rivals, but it was Scarlett who saw Mandy and Anya first.

"They're *baaaack*," she said.

"Anya is registered for a Senior Solo," Bria said as she checked the program. "So at least City Feet isn't lying today."

"Not that we know of," Rochelle pointed out.

Scarlett checked the program to see what else

City Feet was dancing. It was no surprise that Mandy had an acro routine and that Anya was performing ballet. Then she read the name of their group number: "Frenemies Forever."

"What do you think this means?" she asked the girls.

"*Ick!* You don't think Justine is trying to embarrass Toni in front of everyone, do you?" Rochelle asked.

Just then, another person caught Scarlett's eye: Justine. She was standing in the lobby, checking her watch and sipping a cup of coffee.

"She looks like she might be waiting for someone," Rochelle said.

Scarlett remembered the e-mail they had sent. "This is terrible. She and Toni cannot have a showdown right before Nationals!"

"All we have to do is keep Toni away from her," Rochelle explained. "If Toni doesn't show up in the lobby, Justine will just assume she changed her mind."

Bria tugged on Scarlett's elbow: "Don't look now . . ."

There, walking down the hall and just steps away from colliding with Justine, was Miss Toni.

"Quick!" Scarlett said, grabbing her friends. "Hide!"

They ducked under a table covered in leotards and tutus. They could hear everything but hoped neither of the coaches would catch them eavesdropping.

"Toni. You wanted to talk. So I'm here," Justine said.

"What on earth are you talking about?" Toni grumped. "I don't want to talk to you."

"Then why did you send me an e-mail?"

Scarlett gulped and braced herself for Toni's reaction.

"E-mail? I didn't e-mail you. I told you twenty years ago I never wanted to speak to you again. And I meant it."

Scarlett held her breath, waiting for Justine to fire back.

"Are you really going to hold a grudge forever?" Justine asked. "I said I was sorry. It's ancient history. Can't we just be friends?"

Scarlett peeked out from under the table to see Toni's reaction. She didn't look angry. In fact, she looked a little sad.

"When we both were asked to audition for the lead in *Swan Lake*, you told me it was rescheduled. You made sure I couldn't show up for the tryout," Toni said.

"I was scared you were going to beat me. I knew you would; you were better than I was," Justine said softly. "I'm sorry. I was wrong."

Toni shook her head. "You ruined my chances of becoming a principal dancer at ABC, and you ruined our friendship. Now if you'll excuse me, I have to find three girls from my team for rehearsal."

"Poor Toni." Scarlett sighed.

"Poor us!" Rochelle said. "She's going to kill us if we don't get back into rehearsal!"

As they crawled out from under the table, Miss Toni was standing right there, hovering over them.

"You girls have some explaining to do," she said sternly. "But we don't have time now. Get inside—we have only forty-five minutes before the start of the competition. And I am not letting Justine beat us again."

The Divas rehearsed the group routine a dozen times in the dressing room until Scarlett's calves were burning.

"I want it clean and sharp!" Toni commanded. "Liberty, your arms need to come over your head straight. And Bria, you need to run farther downstage, over there. A six and a seven and an eight . . ."

Finally, it was time to get changed into their costumes.

"I don't need to tell you how important this competition is for us," Miss Toni told them. "There are going to be some very important people watching in the audience: talent scouts, agents, Broadway producers. Give it a hundred and ten percent tonight."

Scarlett was sure that Justine was giving her dancers a similar speech. She felt like all the girls were caught in a tug-of-war between the two dance coaches. Back in the dressing room, there was even more drama brewing.

"Scarlett, you have to help me!" Rochelle dragged her over to a corner where an argument was taking place between Rochelle's and Liberty's mothers.

"Honestly, you cannot tell me that you think Zumba is an art form!" Jane Montgomery was saying. "It's a complete waste of time. I would never call it dance!"

"I didn't ask you!" Rochelle's mom protested. "I simply said I was going to teach a Zumba class at Rock's school."

"Well, if you don't want a professional opinion . . . ," Jane said. She stormed off to unzip Liberty's costume from its garment bag.

"See what I mean?" Rochelle said. "It's getting ugly in here, too!"

"Relax." Scarlett patted her on the back. "Everyone is just a little tense because of the competition."

"Oh my gooshness!" she heard Gracie exclaim. Gracie was hovering around Liberty's costume rack, hoping to see her solo costume unveiled.

"Is that for real?" Rochelle gasped when she saw Liberty dressed in a gold lamé leotard covered in dangling strands of nickels, dimes, and quarters.

"The money on it? Yes. It's real," Liberty replied. Her solo was called "Jackpot," and Liberty looked like a human slot machine.

Scarlett cracked up. The costume was truly over the top.

"It's kind of heavy," Liberty complained as her mom secured the straps.

"Well, it's made of coins . . . What did you expect?"

"I can't really move very well in it." She tried to lift one of her arms, but the entire sleeve was dripping in coins. "Mom, this is crazy! It weighs a ton!"

Her mother hurried her out the door. "Deal with it," she said. "You think Katy Perry complains when they dress her in cupcakes? We all must suffer for our art."

Liberty was the last dancer up for Junior Solo. A girl from Move Manhattan went before her—and she had already set the bar high with a nearly flawless lyrical routine.

"Next up, Liberty from Dance Divas, performing a contemporary dance, 'Jackpot.'"

Liberty walked out onstage, the coins on her costume clinking and clanking with every turned-out step.

As the music began, she darted back and forth, then spun out into an *arabesque* turn. A quarter went flying off, landing in a judge's lap.

"Oh my gooshness!" Gracie squealed from the wings. "She's losing her money!"

Another coin landed with a *plunk* on the stage as she did her *grand jeté*; two more as she *chaînéd* across the floor.

By the time the dance was over, Liberty's

costume was certainly lighter. The audience was digging under their seats trying to gather up all the spare change.

"Was that supposed to happen?" Bria asked.

"Let's hope the judges think so," said Liberty's mom, mopping her brow with a pink silk scarf.

Liberty stormed offstage. "I am humiliated!" she wailed. "My entire costume fell apart!"

"Wow," said Mandy, making her way toward the stage for the Petite Solos. "Thanks for the change for the candy machine!" She waved a handful of coins under Liberty's nose. She was dressed in a green velvet jumpsuit for her acro solo, "Leapfrog."

Liberty gritted her teeth. Scarlett was afraid Liberty would do something they'd all regret, so she held Liberty's arm and said cheerfully, "That was so cool! How'd you time the coins to come off at just the right moments like that?"

"You mean, it was on purpose?" Mandy asked.

Liberty picked up where Scarlett left off. "Of course. Do you have any idea how difficult it was to rehearse that routine?"

"It was coin choreography," Scarlett added. "Which is pretty cool, don't you think?"

Mandy nodded slowly. "Yeah, I guess . . ." Then she hopped off to perform her dance.

Liberty looked down at her tattered costume. "Thanks for not making me look any more stupid than I already do," she told Scarlett.

"On the bright side, your turns were amazing," Scarlett said.

"And the judges probably appreciated the tips!" Rochelle chuckled.

CHAPTER 17

Sister Act

Gracie checked her ballet slippers one last time, making sure her Lucky Stars were tucked neatly inside.

"Remember, you're not alone." Scarlett hugged her one last time. "We're right here!" Rochelle, Bria, and Liberty all gave her the thumbs-up.

A voice over the loudspeaker boomed: "Performing an acro routine entitled 'Watch Out, World—Here I Come!' please put your hands together for Gracie from Dance Divas!"

Gracie skipped out onstage and took her position: hands on her hips in a sassy, playful pose.

As the music started, she kicked up her heels, wiggled her butt, and did a split while blowing kisses to the judges.

So far, so good, Scarlett thought. Then she noticed Gracie was still sitting on the floor. She stared at the audience, glassy-eyed and terrified.

"Here we go again," Liberty said.

Scarlett thought quickly. She skipped out onto the stage and twirled around Gracie, pulling her up under her arms to a standing position.

"Gracie, I'm right here!" she whispered in her little sister's ear. "Snap out of it!" As soon as she saw Scarlett by her side, Gracie was fine. Together, they improvised a dance around the stage, leaping and twirling and playing off each other, just like they sometimes did at home in their living room.

At the end, Gracie did her back walkover and the crowd broke into thunderous applause. Their duet was a smashing success!

After almost all the single, duo, and trio performances, it was time for City Feet to take the stage for the group number. The Divas sat right up front to watch (and maybe to psych them out just a little).

The dance featured Phoebe and Mandy, dressed like ballerinas, having a tug-of-war in the center of the stage. The rest of the team danced around them, taking sides and encouraging them to tear at each other's tutus till they were both in shreds. Then one ballerina—Mandy—let go of the rope. She extended a hand, and Anya took it. The dance ended with the girls, arm in arm, strolling offstage.

"It's weird," Bria whispered. "I don't get it."

"Do you think Toni does?" Scarlett asked. She glanced at the seat Toni had been in all afternoon. It was empty.

"Be right back. Forgot something in my bag," Scarlett said, squeezing past the girls in their seats. She ducked out the door of the main stage and looked around the lobby. There, just as she had hoped, was Miss Toni.

"You missed City Feet's group dance," she said softly to her teacher.

"I saw it," she replied. She patted the ledge where she was seated so Scarlett would join her.

"Justine and I were once as close as sisters," she explained. "We would have done anything for each other—just like you did today for Gracie."

Scarlett gulped. "Sorry about that. I didn't know what else to do."

"You did the right thing—even if your choreography wasn't so polished," Miss Toni said, and smiled.

"Do you think you will ever be friends with Justine again?" Scarlett asked.

Toni shrugged. "I don't know. But she taught me a valuable lesson back at ABC. She taught me the meaning of friendship."

Scarlett looked puzzled. "I thought she stabbed you in the back at the *Swan Lake* audition?"

Toni nodded. "She did. And I knew I would never do that to a friend. No matter how much I wanted to win. I try to teach that to you girls all the time. A team is only as strong as the sum of its individual parts."

Scarlett nodded. "City Feet's dance was pretty amazing."

"My Divas are pretty amazing—and I don't just mean on the dance floor," Toni said softly. "Thanks for trying to patch things up between me and Justine. Let's just say it's a work in progress." She stood up and headed for the main hall.

"You coming?" She winked at Scarlett. "I hear there's this team called Dance Divas that's about to perform."

Scarlett smiled. "Wouldn't miss it for the world!"

CHAPTER 18

Cop and Robbers

Scarlett adjusted the brim of her silver sequined fedora. "Do I look like a gangster?" she asked her mom backstage. She made her toughest bad-guy face.

"You look great!" her mom said, chuckling. "You, too, Gracie."

Gracie was wearing an old-fashioned "cop" costume, complete with a police hat and a shiny silver badge pinned to her black velvet leotard. Both Liberty and Bria were dressed like "gangster molls" in white-fringed flapper dresses and short black-bobbed wigs.

"You guys look like Bonnie and Clyde." Rochelle's mom gushed. She made sure Rochelle's pin-striped suit jacket was buttoned over her leotard. "I love it!"

Behind the curtains, Miss Toni rolled their props onto the stage. There was a bank-safe door and bags of money that were stuffed with fake dollar bills.

"Watch your legs on the back *attitude*," Toni reminded them. "And I want to see emotion in your faces—not just in your bodies. Clear?"

Scarlett heard the emcee announce their number: "Please welcome the Dance Divas performing a Broadway-style dance entitled 'The Untouchables'!"

Red lights flashed and sirens shrieked as Scarlett and Rochelle raced onstage and "stole" bags of money from the bank safe. They leaped across the floor, narrowly "escaping" Gracie, the policeman, who cartwheeled from one end of the stage to the other.

Liberty and Bria *pirouetted* in perfect synch,

their fringed skirts spinning wildly. At the end of the number, the four girls burst out of the bank safe and fired confetti cannons at the audience. A net suddenly fell from the ceiling, "capturing" the criminals. Gracie did a front walkover and raised her hands over her head in victory.

The audience jumped to their feet in a standing ovation. "That was awesome!" Rochelle said breathlessly as they took their bows. Scarlett agreed. It was by far the best dance routine the Divas had ever performed. But would it be enough to beat City Feet?

The judges deliberated for thirty minutes before summoning all the contestants to the stage to announce the results. Scarlett felt strangely calm. She knew they had done their very best, and that meant more than any trophy or title.

"In the Petite Solo category, first place goes to 'Leapfrog,' by Mandy Hammond from City Feet Dance Studio!" Mandy hopped back onstage and claimed her prize.

Scarlett saw the disappointment on Gracie's face.

"She probably has warts, Gracie," she joked. "Get it? Frog? Warts?"

Anya took first place for Teen Solo. That was two top titles already for City Feet.

"Next up, the Junior Solo awards," said the announcer.

Liberty hung her head. "I'm never gonna win," she said. Scarlett had never seen her act humble.

"Don't say that." She tried to reassure Liberty. "It was just a silly wardrobe malfunction. Every star has them."

Liberty looked into her eyes. "Yeah, but I'm not a star," she said softly. "My mom wants me to be, but I'm not Katy Perry or Beyoncé."

"Not even Lady Gaga?" Rochelle teased.

"No," Liberty replied. Scarlett saw there were tears in her eyes. She put an arm around her.

"No, you're not. You're Liberty—and we like you just the way you are."

"We do?" Rochelle asked.

Scarlett shot her a look. "We do. Right, Divas?"

They all nodded and hugged. The emcee was

holding the envelope in his hand with the first-place winner inside. "No matter what happens, Liberty, you have us on your team," Scarlett said.

"In first place, in the Junior Solo division, 'Jackpot,' by Liberty Montgomery, Dance Divas Studio!"

Liberty looked positively shocked. Scarlett practically had to drag her to her feet to accept her trophy. But once the crown was on her head, the announcer had a hard time getting her to leave the stage so he could read the duo results!

"Please take a seat, Liberty," he said into the mike. "Liberty, thank you. Please sit down!" Liberty blew kisses to the audience and reluctantly sat back down.

Since Dance Divas had no duos, Scarlett was barely paying attention when the emcee read, "In third place, Junior Duo, Gracie and Scarlett Borden, 'Watch Out, World—Here I Come!'—Dance Divas Studio!"

"What?" She gasped. "We won for *Duo*? Gracie, did you hear that? We won!"

"You guys were a great sister act." Rochelle beamed. "Now go get your trophy."

Gracie ran up to the emcee and practically yanked the trophy from his hands. "Look! My first dance trophy!" she told Scarlett. "I mean, *ours*."

Scarlett bent over and gave her a hug. "Nope, you deserve this one all by yourself for being so brave. And there'll be lots more. Just wait and see!"

Once all the individual prizes had been awarded, it was time for the group titles. This was the moment that all the dance coaches had been waiting for. Both Toni and Justine were sitting in the front row. This time, Scarlett had no trouble reading her teacher's face. It was beaming with pride and confidence.

Third place went to a Pittsburgh dance company. "No surprise there." Rochelle sniffed. "They have their own TV show!" When the judge opened the next envelope, he looked surprised.

"Well, I have never seen this in a National competition before," he said. "Only one-tenth of a point separates our first- and second-place winners."

Scarlett closed her eyes and held her breath. Gracie leaned over and whispered in her ear, "Let's both make a wish on our Lucky Stars."

"In second place: 'Frenemies Forever,' City Feet Dance Studio. And in first place: 'The Untouchables,' Dance Divas Studio!"

The audience went wild. Miss Toni hugged and congratulated all the Dance Divas moms in the audience.

The trophy was over five feet tall—taller than Gracie—and it weighed a ton. It took all five girls to lift it in the air.

Mandy, Anya, Phoebe, and the rest of the City Feet team offered a congratulatory cheer: "Two-four-six-eight, who do we appreciate? DIVAS! DIVAS! DANCE DIVAS!"

"That's nice," Bria said. But she spoke too soon. Mandy climbed on top of a pyramid of her teammates and added, "Eight-six-four-two, next time we are beating you! CITY FEET! CITY FEET! Go, CITY FEET!"

Liberty rolled her eyes. "Let 'em bring it. We're the best dance team in the country—and we've got the trophy to prove it."

"You don't need a trophy to prove it." Miss Toni had joined them onstage to celebrate. "I knew it all along."

As the girls packed their bags and boarded the bus, Scarlett couldn't help feeling a little sad that the competition was over. As nerve-racking as it had been, it had brought the team even closer together. Liberty even let Gracie nap on her poodle pillow pet.

Their first-place trophy took up an entire seat next to Miss Toni.

"I'm looking forward to a little R & R now that this is all over," Liberty's mom said. "Maybe a vacation in Saint Barts . . . or Saint-Tropez?"

"I'm looking forward to sleeping in late tomorrow!" Scarlett's mom added. "How about you, Toni?"

Toni let her hair down out of her tight ballet

bun. "I'm taking a few winks on the way home," she replied. "We start rehearsals for the next competition bright and early tomorrow morning."

The moms all groaned, but Scarlett smiled. There was no place in the world she would rather be than at Dance Divas Studio.

Glossary of Dance Terms

Arabesque: a move where the dancer stands on one leg with the other leg extended behind her at 90 degrees.

Attitude: a pose in which one leg is raised in back or in front with the knee bent.

Battement: a quick kick either high (grand battement) or low (petit battement).

Chaîné: a series of quick turns.

Développé: a move where the dancer unfolds her leg in the air.

Fouetté: a turning step where the leg whips out to the side.

Grand jeté: a large forward leap in the air that looks like a flying split.

Pirouette: a turn on one leg with the other leg behind.

Rond de jambe: a move where the dancer makes halfcircles with one leg.

Sauté: a jump using one or two legs.

Sheryl Berk is a proud ballet mom and a *New York Times* bestselling author. She has collaborated with numerous celebrities on their memoirs, including Britney Spears, *Glee*'s Jenna Ushkowitz, and *Shake It Up*'s Zendaya. Her book with Bethany Hamilton, *Soul Surfer*, hit #1 on the *New York Times* bestseller list and became a major motion picture. She is also the author of The Cupcake Club book series with her ten-year-old daughter, Carrie.